Cage the Lie

by David Myers

DORRANCE
PUBLISHING CO
EST. 1920
PITTSBURGH, PENNSYLVANIA 15238

Dorrance Publishing Co
585 Alpha Drive
Pittsburgh, PA 15238
Visit our website at *www.dorrancebookstore.com*

ISBN: 979-8-89211-115-7
eISBN: 979-8-89211-613-8

1
Disaster Strikes

Serena Mae, a police officer for the small town of Brisbon, woke up on the morning of her promotion. She was about to become a sergeant, a position open to her because her boyfriend, Sergeant Willy Breckenridge, was being promoted to lieutenant on that same day. Willy had been a shift commander for several years and was now looking forward to becoming a watch commander. He was excited to turn over the reins of shift commander to his girlfriend, Serena, as she, in his eyes, was the best qualified for the promotion.

Serena took her morning jog, a four-mile run through the rundown districts in Brisbon, where friendly waves from friendly business owners showed Serena how much she was appreciated by the community. She wanted to stop and inform the public of her promotion but did not want to break her stride and tax her breathing. So, she was satisfied to simply wave and say hi, realizing that the next time the neighborhood business owners saw her, she would be wearing stripes on her sleeve.

After her morning shower, she made her way to the police department, where at 10 a.m. she would be officially named Sergeant Serena Mae Morris. Upon her arrival, she observed that the station was almost vacant. Realizing that this was unusual this time of day, she made her way to the office of the chief of police. Chief Larry

Breckenridge, brother of Willy, motioned Serena into her office. He was notably excited, breathing labored, and tears in his eyes.

"Chief, aren't you a bit overly excited about your brother's and my promotion?" she joked.

"No joke, Serena, Willy was shot about fifteen minutes ago during a routine traffic stop. Get in my car, we are going to the ER. He's not expected to make it!" Chief Breckenridge anxiously exclaimed.

They raced to the hospital, siren blazing, lights flashing, weaving in and out of traffic.

Suddenly over the police radio, a police officer named Rodriguez stated, "Suspect in custody."

A terrified Serena asked, "What happened, Chief?"

"Routine traffic stop on Clark Avenue near 7th Street. Willy approached the vehicle when the driver turned on him and fired two shots. One in the chest and one in the shoulder. Willy went down and an eyewitness had to call us. The witness had the license plate and color of the car, as well as direction of travel."

"But… but why? Was the shooter wanted? Did he have warrants?" asked Serena, trying to make sense of it all.

"I don't know. But the he is a she. Rodriguez has her in custody. The witness said it was a woman."

They rushed into the ER and were escorted immediately to Willy. Chief Breckenridge asked the escorting nurse how his brother was doing, but no answer was given. They arrived at Willy's room where they observed a doctor pulling the bedsheet over Willy's face.

"No. No!" Serena moaned in distress. "No!" she shouted.

"No! Not Willy," the chief lamented. "Not my little brother!"

Four days later, the funeral and burial of Willy was attended by almost the entire police force as well as the community. The media covered the day's events and was in a frenzy because this was the first death of a policeman on duty in the history of Brisbon. Serena stayed close to the chief and found herself leaning on him during the burial.

The chief, realizing how hard Willy's death had hit Serena, had given Serena as much time off as she needed since the shooting. He had taken three days off himself to collect his thoughts and regain focus. The investigation into Willy's death was completed; all the paperwork filed with the attorney general's office and the suspect incarcerated in the county jail. All that was left was for the AG office to file charges and for the court to schedule the trial date. The motive for the shooting was still unclear. The detectives assigned to the case were closed-mouthed until they had all the facts.

After the funeral, Serena went home and found a sea of reporters waiting for her. She stepped out of the vehicle where she suffered through a barrage of questions ranging from personal to professional. "Was Sergeant Breckenridge your fiancé? Your boyfriend? Were you planning on getting married? How do you feel about the woman who shot him? Are you back at work?"

Serena avoided all the questions simply by responding, "No comment," and then asked and then demanded the media leave her property. She threatened to have the fire department spray them with water if they persisted on her property. This encouraged the media to move to the sidewalk - public property.

Grief-stricken and in tears, Serena sobbed at the loss of her co-worker and boyfriend. The chief ordered officers to drive by her house periodically after he hadn't heard from her in a few weeks. Some of the roving patrols stopped to check on her, while others simply drove by, honking the car horn. The community left meals and cards on her porch and left their phone numbers in the event she needed anything.

About a month had passed before Serena was seen outside her house. She opened the door and helped the delivery driver carry her groceries into her house and then back into the house for another extended period of time.

Finally the trial was set, and trial day had arrived. Serena once again sat next to the chief and leaned on him for support. The judge asked the defendant's court-appointed attorney whether she was pleading guilty or not guilty, to which the attorney replied "guilty." The attorney then informed the judge that the defendant, a Miss Melony Sanderson, wished to waive her right to a trial by jury. This caused a stir in the courtroom, to which the judge was able to maintain order by pounding his gavel. The state had no objections, and so a sentencing was scheduled in two months.

On the way out of the courthouse, the chief and Serena were engaged in a conversation. A weepy Serena expressed that she still needed to find closure and needed more time. The chief understood and said he had to get to a media interview and would talk to her later.

The next two months Serena slowly began to get back into a routine. She started jogging again and would tear up only when the local business owners and others expressed their support and love for her. She ventured to the grocery store, an occasional fast-food visit, and a couple of long rides in the country. Although still grieving, her tears were fewer than before, and her drive was strengthening. She was finding it a little easier to talk with people and was learning how to cope with her loss. She jogged her usual route, but this time stopped at businesses to pay her respects and offer her thanks to all those who were supporting her during these trying times.

The day of sentencing for Miss Melony Sanderson arrived, and a stronger Serena arrived at the courthouse. The judge asked Miss Melony Sanderson if she had anything to say before sentencing or if she had any remorse for her actions.

Miss Sanderson boldly said, "Yeah, I have something to say. I hate cops, and if given another chance, I would do it again!"

Serena sat unmoved. She became stiff-lipped and stoic. She realized her position on the force, and in that moment knew it was time to return to duty. She looked at the chief and observed his face, a squared-off jaw, prominently raised up high and proud. His eyes focused on the defendant and then the judge, the chief squirmed in his seat. Serena could only imagine what the chief, Willy's brother, was thinking. She remained expressionless and restrained.

The judge spoke up, "Since the defendant has expressed no remorse, and since the defendant insists she would do this heinous act of cowardice again, the court finds the defendant guilty of capital murder, and hereby sentences the defendant, Miss Melony Sanderson, to life in prison with no possibility of parole. The defendant will be remanded into the custody of the department of corrections. Court is adjourned." And with the pound of the gavel, the sentencing was complete.

As Serena walked out of the courtroom, a sense of guilt descended on her. She suddenly realized that with all the tragedy, she never once asked the chief how he was doing. She made Willy's death all about her, never even giving a thought to anyone else. She made her way to the chief and asked him how he was holding out.

The chief insisted he was fine, and that his mother was taking this pretty hard. "After all," he said, "it was I who let her baby boy die!"

"Oooh, that's rough," Serena replied. "Anything I can do?"

"No. Mom will come around. She's speaking out of loss and emotion. Deep down I know she doesn't blame me. Just have to give it time. So, how are you?"

"I'm ready to come back to work," replied Serena.

"Okay. You think you are ready?" the chief asked.

"Yes. I'm good to go."

"Okay. I'll tell you what. Come tomorrow morning. I will partner you up with Officer Helmsley. I want someone with you for a week or two just to be sure you are good to go. Any problem with that?"

"No, Chief. I guess not," Serena responded.

"Once I get a positive report from him, I'll let you go solo. We still have that sergeant position open. If in a couple months you feel like you are still up for it, it's yours. I've been saving it for you, Officer Morris."

"Yes sir, Chief," responded Serena. "Will be in tomorrow morning."

Serena drove home and immediately understood why the chief was pairing her up with Helmsley. Helmsley was the primary training officer for the department and a twelve-year veteran. The rookies out of the police academy would be assigned to him for six weeks after graduation. He would train them on the expectations of the Brisbon P.D., the quirks of the community, situational enforcement, and shoot or don't shoot situations. He was a good judge of character and understood how to guide rookies into making good decisions. He had proven himself over and over again whether in the process of training or out cruising by himself. He had no desire to become a supervisor. His whole life was the department, the job he had worked hard to acquire, and the trust the chief put in him to train the rookies and help fix their deficiencies. He was single, focused, and loved being a cop. Serena had no doubt he would see she was squared away and ready to resume her role on the Brisbon PD. She looked forward to spending a week with her former training officer from six years back.

2
FLYING SOLO

The next two weeks were rather uneventful. Traffic stops, shop-lifters, motor vehicle accidents, welfare checks, noise complaints, and road construction detail were the major calls handled by Serena and Helmsley. On the Thursday of week two, a call came in for domestic violence. Helmsley and Serena approached the apartment in question and found a drunk man brandishing a knife. The woman who called the police lived with this man and had managed her way to the apartment parking lot. Serena approached the man with Helmsley in tow. She reasoned with this man, as best you could with someone inebriated to the point he was, and talked him into surrendering his knife. Serena arrested him without incident and the two of them transported him to jail. The next day the chief released Serena from her leash and let her patrol by herself.

Days turned into weeks as Serena patrolled in what seemed like an endless symposium of routine calls. Serena's attitude toward this was consistent - a boring day at work means she is going home safe and sound. The weeks turned into months before Serena was called into the chief's office. In his office, she was given her long-awaited promotion. There, sewn on a brand-new uniform shirt, were her sergeant stripes. Sergeant Serena Mae Morris exited the chief's office to applause and offers of congratulations from her co-workers and now subordinates. As she drove home that day, tears flooded her eyes at the thought of her late boyfriend, Sergeant Willy Breckenridge.

That evening, a rainy, dark, cloudy night, Serena decided to celebrate her promotion. She entered a small club known for its good food, good music, and upscale crowd. She seated herself at the bar and struck up a conversation with the bartender. Serena was an expert in small talk, a trait she developed over the years in her profession. She heard and then observed a commotion at the entrance door, where she saw a young man in his mid-twenties slip and fall as he entered the Ace of Clubs. A club employee and she rushed over to the man to help him up and to see if he was alright.

"I'm fine," he said. "Just wet outside and my shoes are slick."

"Are you sure you're okay?" asked the club employee.

"Yes, I'm good. No worse for the wear."

Serena looked at the man and suddenly observed he had a 9mm handgun stashed in his belt. Serena asked the man if he had a permit to carry a concealed weapon.

"What are you, a cop or something?" he demanded.

"Well, actually I am," she responded. "Sergeant Morris. Now, do you have a permit?"

"Yes, I do." The man reached into his back pocket and removed his wallet. He then produced a CCW permit and handed it to Serena.

She studied it carefully and saw his name was Grant Fitzgerald, Private Investigator, and that the picture matched his face. "Well, Mr. Fitzgerald, it looks like everything checks out."

"Please, call me Fitz, that's what everyone calls me." He sat in the seat next to Serena and was offered a beer by the bartender.

"On the house, of course," stated the bartender.

"Hi Sergeant," said Fitz, "do you have a first name?"

"Serena."

"Hello Serena. I suppose the police officer in you is wondering what I am doing in your town," Fitz responded.

"The thought did cross my mind, especially since you are carrying that piece in your belt," Serena replied.

"Fair enough. I have been hired by a local woman to find someone. I always carry it because just like your line of work, mine can be dangerous as well. This job may prove to be the riskiest. Time will tell."

A contemptuous Serena replied, "Have you given thought to collaborating with the police on this? You know, leave it to the pros?"

"No. No way. Don't need the police sticking their noses into my business. No offense, Sarge!"

"Okay. Don't say I didn't ask. Stay out of trouble. Step out of line with that piece and we'll be right on your tail," Serena responded flatly.

With that, Serena left the Ace of Clubs and went home. The next day Serena visited Willy's gravesite. She placed flowers near the headstone and thought to herself, *He was a good man. I miss you, Willy.*

The next few weeks, Serena adjusted to her new position and attended a three-day seminar on supervision. She had no experience in that area, so she was happy to learn the basics of supervising people. She knew she had a good group of subordinates, and she was eager to help them in every way possible. She was thankful to be supervising Officer Rodriguez because he arrested Willy's killer, and she was thankful to be supervising Officer Helmsley, as he brought a sense of composure in any situation. In total, she was responsible for eight officers, six of them experienced and only two with maybe a year of experience. Every one of them—Helmsley trained.

On her next day off, Serena went on a date with Helmsley's brother Bo. She wasn't exactly in favor of dating the brother or even a friend of someone she supervises, but she agreed to dating Bo as kind of a favor to Officer Helmsley. It was a blind date that saw the two of them meet at an off the grid restaurant called Off the Grid, located in the neighboring town of Lancaster. Serena arrived and was led to a table already occupied by Bo. She said hi to him as she sat down and couldn't help but think, *Not bad!*

"I feel like I already know you. My brother has told me so much about you," said Bo.

"Oh? Hopefully all good," Serena responded sarcastically. "I don't know anything about you."

"Well, I'm the vice president of First Bank, Main Street here in Lancaster. I started as a teller at the age of eighteen about eleven years ago. Before that, I worked odd jobs in high school… Oh, I'm sorry. I don't mean to sound like a job resume!"

"That's okay, I want to know. What are your hobbies, if any?" asked Serena.

"I love fishing and hunting. I enjoy traveling and hope to fish in Alaska one day. I attended college part time the last seven years and finally managed to acquire my bachelor's degree in business administration."

"I see. Congratulations. Sounds like you like to stay busy and active. I do as well," Serena replied.

Their dinner conversation remained unimaginative, unimpressive, and business-like.

When the date finally ended, Bo explained apologetically to Serena that he wasn't in favor of going on a blind date with her. "I did it as a favor to my brother."

"What a coincidence," Serena interjected, "same here."

"Okay, so where do we go from here?" asked Bo.

"Good question. I don't exactly know," Serena responded.

"How about we start over. I'll give you a call next week, ask you for a date, and you can decide then if you will accept my request. No hard feelings if you say no. But honestly Serena, I hope you'll give me a second chance. Now that we've met, we may find we have things in common and maybe a connection."

"No, I don't think so," replied Serena.

Bo's face turned downcast.

"I'd rather we finish this date and then you ask me for a second before the night is over. I would much prefer to tell you yes or no to your face."

"Okay. Sounds great." With that, Bo offered his hand to Serena, and said, "Hi. I'm Bo. It's a pleasure to meet you. How about we take a walk along the beach and get to know each other?"

They both chuckled as Bo led her out the door and to the beach.

$$3$$

Prank Call?

A couple of days later a call rang out from Sgt. Morris' patrol car radio for shots fired, location was the top tier of the parking garage on Mendell Avenue. When she arrived, officers Rodriguez and Helmsley were already on the scene and investigating. Officer Rodriguez was talking to a man in a black overcoat and black shoes. The man turned around and saw Sergeant Morris approaching on foot.

As soon as she saw him, she stated, "Fitz, is that you?"

"It sure is," replied Fitz, "what's all the commotion?"

Officer Rodriguez spoke up and told Fitz, "Like I was telling you, dispatch received a call of shots fired at this location." He turned to Sergeant Morris. "When I arrived, this man, Fitz, as you refer to him, was the only one on scene."

Sergeant Morris held out her hand and ordered Fitz to turn it over. Fitz reached into his belt and pulled out his firearm. He gave it to Sergeant Morris who felt the barrel and checked to see if it had been fired. It all checked out.

"It's not hot. There are no empty cases on the ground and the magazine clip is fully loaded." She then asked Fitz, "How long have you been here?"

Fitz replied, "About fifteen minutes."

"Did you hear a gunshot?"

Again Fitz, "No, ma'am, no gunshots."

"Why are you here?" asked the Sergeant.

"My investigation has led me here. But my lead did not pan out. I was just heading back to my car when you guys showed up," Fitz muttered.

Sergeant Morris and Fitz sat down in her squad car as the other two officers continued the investigation. Helmsley observed that his sergeant and Fitz were having a heated discussion, but he was unable to hear what was being said. In a few minutes, Fitz exited the patrol car and drove away in his own car.

Sgt. Morris explained to Helmsley and Rodriguez how and where she met Private Investigator Fitzgerald. She had to let him go today because she had nothing on him to warrant detaining him any longer. She told both of them that there is something unscrupulous about Fitz and to be aware he has a CCW and a handgun on him.

"I just don't trust him!"

The remainder of Serena's shift seemed to pass by slowly. She seemed overly focused on the shots fired call, and she knew it. It troubled her that the only person at the location was Fitz, and he denied hearing anything. She reasoned that perhaps Fitz had another handgun on him that she missed. What were the chances of that? After a lot of thought, the chances for that seemed to multiply.

When Serena arrived home that evening, she saw her message machine blinking. It was Bo asking if she was up for a third date this coming Saturday. He suggested a square dance at a friend's barn or miniature golf. That Saturday the two of them played a round of miniature golf and then took a drive. The conversation was light as they parked by the lake. As the sun set, Bo reached over, took Serena's hand, and kissed her. This caught Serena by surprise, but she did not pull back. Bo recognized he caught her by surprise and ended the kiss abruptly. She scootched herself over toward him on the front seat, and they relaxed and watched the sun set. Both of them wondered if this was the beginning of something or if the awkwardness of the kiss would prevent Bo from attempting another. Maybe not tonight, but at some point. Serena understood she was dating someone inexperienced and shy, and she was quite okay with that. She just had lost Willy and preferred to move slowly, so Bo seemed to fit the bill.

Dropping Serena off at her house, Bo did not walk her to the door. He chastised himself the rest of the evening for that 'smooth move' as well as for the awkwardness of the kiss, and really for the entire evening. *I can only imagine what kind of a nincompoop she thinks I am*, Bo thought to himself.

Serena was also surprised that Bo did not walk her to the door and at least attempted another kiss, maybe just a peck on the cheek. She surmised that *maybe he's just not into me*. Immediately, her sense of logic took over, leading her to once again recognize that Bo simply isn't a lady's man but more of a beginner with women. She did ponder, however, how it was possible that a twenty-nine-year-old man knew nothing about women or how to engage with a woman. She decided that if he did ask her out again, maybe she would take the lead in the romance department. Perhaps this would give him confidence to realize he has a shot with her. *Slow is one thing, but inert is egregious*, she thought.

The next day "Shots fired!" blurted over Sgt. Morris' patrol car radio. "Location upper tier parking garage on Mendell Avenue."

"Same place as last time," Officer Rodriguez said to himself.

As he raced to the parking garage, lights flashing and siren wailing, he heard on the police radio that Officer Barnes was responding as back-up. Kimberly Barnes had just completed her training with Helmsley and was experiencing her second week in a patrol car by herself. She was a short, fit woman with a 'go get 'em' attitude and a gung-ho disposition. Shots fired was a call that excited Barnes and was the reason she got into police work. Sgt. Morris radioed that she would get there as soon as she could but was currently in the process of transporting a felony arrestee to the county jail.

Rodriguez arrived first with Barnes in tow. They searched the area for the caller, the perpetrator, and any signs of shots fired. Like the first time, they found nothing. Sgt. Morris arrived fully expecting Fitz to be at the scene, but to her dismay, he was not. A further and more thorough check of the surrounding area revealed nothing.

About a half hour later, the squad cars departed. Ten minutes after that, when the coast was sure to be clear, Fitz climbed out from inside a dumpster located on the top tier of the parking structure. He brushed himself off and ran down two levels to his car. Jumping in, he casually made his way out of the parking structure.

Approximately three minutes later, Sgt. Morris recognized Fitz's car and proceeded to pull him over. Fitz explained he was out and about only to find somewhere to eat dinner. Sgt. Morris sent him on his way after an in-depth discussion and interrogation. Fitz drove away feeling a huge sense of relief.

Before Sgt. Morris drove away, the chief drove up and parked his squad behind Sgt. Morris. Sgt. Morris explained everything about the two shots fired calls to the chief, as well as how she met Fitz.

The chief sternly reprimanded Sgt. Morris for not following protocol, as she failed to notify the watch commander about Fitz. "Next time you follow procedure Sergeant, you understand? Furthermore, any private investigator working in our district is required to notify us of his business in the city. You failed to advise him of this, did you not?"

"Yes, Chief, I did," replied a despondent Morris.

"Okay, Sergeant. When you locate him, I want to have a talk with him. No two-bit P.I. is going to disrupt our town." Having scolded Morris, the chief sped away.

Sgt. Morris, although distraught after the words of the chief, knew he was right. She failed to follow established protocol and procedure. Somewhere along the way she made the decision, consciously or unconsciously, that she could handle this situation on her own. Now, epic failure! She ended her shift on a sad note, and worse yet, was unable to locate Fitz for the chief. The remainder of the shift was nothing more than a clock slowly ticking away the time. She knew she was sulking and was doing her best to get over it but found herself brooding like a whining child.

At home, Serena prepared dinner for herself.

"Sloppy joes for sloppy work," she muttered.

At that moment, her telephone rang.

"Hello."

"Hi, Serena," a nervous voice said. "It's me, Bo."

"Hi, Bo, how are you?"

"I'm fine. If you're not busy right now, I thought I might come over and pick you up. The high school drama club is putting on a play, a musical. Would you like to go?" asked Bo.

"No, I don't think so. I'm not really up for a play. But you are welcome to come over and we could watch a movie or something," Serena suggested. "I have sloppy joes we could eat."

"Hmm! Sloppy joes. You drive a hard bargain!" Bo said facetiously. "Be right over."

Serena quickly changed her clothes, brushed her hair, applied some makeup, and changed her shoes. Suddenly, her sullenness turned to eagerness and exhilaration. She decided that tonight she would cure Bo of his shyness. When she answered the doorbell, Bo stood on her doorstep, flowers in hand, wearing jeans and cowboy boots, and a look on his face she had not seen before. *This is a good sign*, she thought.

Bo complimented her on her appearance, saying she looked beautiful, complimented her outfit, and boldly stated, "Can I kiss you? I don't think I can wait another second!"

She nodded her head yes, and Bo immediately grabbed her around the waist and gently pulled her closer and began kissing her. The only thing Serena could think was *What has gotten into him tonight? I think I like it!*

When Sgt. Morris returned to work the following day, she was summoned to the chief's office.

"Why didn't you tell me that Fitz checked in with Lieutenant Baker the first night he arrived in town?" asked the chief.

"Well, I..."

The chief interrupted her. "We could have avoided that whole ordeal the other night had you told me you followed protocol with this Fitz guy. Lt. Baker informed me this morning that Fitz came across you at the Ace of Clubs, and afterwards he checked in with the lieutenant upon your direction."

"Well, Fitz followed through then, I guess," Serena said.

"Okay. Let's get back to work. Be safe!"

"Thanks, Chief," Serena said as she exited his office. *What just happened? I never told Fitz to check in with Lieutenant Baker. I never...* Her thoughts trailed off as she entered her patrol car, and then picked up again. *I need to find him... find out what he is up to and why he lied in my favor.*

Unfortunately for Serena, she came up empty in her attempt to locate Fitz. The entire shift between calls she searched for him. In fact, she had all her on-duty officers search for him as well, but all for naught. She was able to draw only one conclusion: he must have fallen off the face of the earth!

The following weekend, after planning a trip, Serena traveled out of state to her parents' house. She hadn't seen Carl and Rhoda since Willy's funeral, so she made the 200-mile trip to Boston to visit them. Carl was an over-the-road truck driver and was home this weekend. Rhoda, her mother, was a museum curator and was anxious to see her only daughter. Serena arrived, made the usual greetings to parents whom she loved, and was abruptly introduced to a young man named Stuart. Stuart, as Serena soon learned, was invited to be a blind date for Serena. Rhoda had arranged a meeting for the two of them. Stuart, the son of a friend of Rhoda and Carl's, a tall, muscular man, worked for the Massachusetts Game and Fish Department as a wildlife biologist. When Serena and Stuart met, the physical attraction was obvious to both of them.

After visiting with her parents for a while, Serena and Stuart decided to go on their date. Serena was a little apprehensive, mainly because she and Bo enjoyed a great date the last time she had seen him. Bo was a short guy who finally jumped out of his shell. She enjoyed kissing him and was eager to get to know him better, but he had nothing on Stuart. Stuart, a big, strong, athletic man, an outdoors man with a very fit physique, a man that Serena suddenly could see herself falling in love with. She dismissed that feeling as childish, a feeling she felt was nothing more than a physical attraction, with no proof of authenticity until she got to know him.

That evening they went for a small dinner, followed by a walk in a local park, and then to a fancy club for drinks and dancing. Stuart admittedly could not dance but did enjoy the physical contact with Serena during slow dances. Serena was no worse for the wear either. She enjoyed his muscular arms wrapped around her, and appreciated the fact that he was gentle and a gentleman in his interactions with her.

As the evening ended, Stuart drove Serena back to her parents' house. They exchanged phone numbers, and Stuart promised to call Serena in the next day or two. As they stepped into the house, Stuart made a point to look both ways, down the hallway to the left, and into the kitchen to the right, and realizing the coast was clear, he quickly folded his arms around Serena's waist and pulled her close. Serena did not resist; rather, she moved toward him with eager lips in anticipation of what she knew would be the most spectacular kiss she ever received. She was not disappointed. She drove back to Brisbon the next day and wondered to whom her next steps would draw her, Bo or Stuart?

The next two weeks for Sgt. Morris proved to be lackluster and mundane. It seemed like Serena's entire shifts consisted of traffic tickets, gas station drive-aways without paying, and minor disturbances at restaurants and bars. Fitz was constantly on Serena's mind, but nowhere near as much as Bo and Stuart. She decided she would continue to date both of them, understanding that they had little chance of meeting each other because of the distance between the two of them.

She hadn't heard from Bo in about a week, so she was happy when he finally called. Tonight, he would take her to a restaurant opening and then ballroom dancing. Neither one of them knew how to ballroom dance, but Bo was one to try anything once. The goal was to watch other dancers and then give it a whirl themselves. Serena wondered if Stuart would ever take her on such a date. No matter, she felt like each man gave her different experiences, and as far as she was concerned, she was relishing the best of both worlds.

Awkwardness struck almost immediately at the restaurant. Just as they began eating, Serena's cellphone rang. Of course, it was Stuart. Serena excused herself from the table and made a dash to the ladies' room. Stuart wanted to talk for a bit, but Serena told him she couldn't talk now as she was heading for a meeting at the police station. She asked him to call her back later tonight. Stuart felt a little put-off, but agreed to call her at 11:00. Serena returned to her date with Bo and made a quick apology, citing it was work on the phone and it was quite confidential. Not any the wiser, Bo accepted her excuse and the date continued. At about 10:30, Serena asked Bo to take her home from dancing as she was tired and not feeling well. As Bo drove her home, Serena realized this wasn't going to be as easy as she thought. Lying to both men, she realized, was uncomfortable and unsustainable and could only lead to disaster. Serena sat with her phone by her side until 1 a.m., but Stuart never called.

4
Shots Fired

"Shots fired!" rang out, "Location the top tier of the parking structure on Mendell Avenue."

Officer Rodriguez was first on scene. Officer Barnes radioed she was enroute for backup about two minutes out. Sgt. Morris echoed her response but about three minutes out. Rodriguez parked his patrol car in the middle of the entrance to the top tier and exited his vehicle. As he searched for expended casings or any evidence of any criminal activity, he found himself under fire. The shots' point of origin was the dumpster on the top tier.

Retreating in a zig-zag pattern, he high-tailed it toward his squad car and screamed over his hand-held radio, "Officer needs assistance, I'm under fire!"

Returning his call, Officer Barnes responded, "Hang in there, Rod, I'm thirty seconds away!" As Barnes turned the corner to the top tier and barely missing Rodrigez's squad, she forced her vehicle between the dumpster and Rodriguez. Her car now taking the cracking of the gunfire, she and Rodriguez took up position on the opposite side of the squad and returned fire at the dumpster. Sgt. Morris, now rounding the corner and weaving around both squads, immediately assessed the situation and pointed her car directly at the dumpster. Five seconds later, she rammed her car into the dumpster. The dumpster jolted from its position, and then a scream was heard, followed by a thud. Then a loud moan from inside. Sgt. Morris exited her vehicle and motioned for Rodriguez and Barnes to climb atop the hood of her patrol car.

With weapons drawn, both officers did as directed while Sgt. Morris provided cover from the side of the dumpster.

Barnes yelled out, "Gun!"

Rodriguez jumped into the dumpster, secured the loose gun, and placed handcuffs on the perp.

Barnes sounded out "Code 4," and Sgt. Morris holstered her firearm, as did Barnes.

The three of them dragged the perpetrator over the side and out of the dumpster.

Rodriguez read him his Miranda rights when Sgt. Morris screamed out, "Fitz!"

At that moment, shots rang out once again; this time from behind. Sgt. Morris grabbed Fitz and shuffled him to a safe location behind Officer Barnes' patrol car. Barnes and Rodriguez grabbed the unidentified dumpster driver and dragged him to safety as well. Shots continued to spray Barnes' car. Sgt. Morris called for backup as she and the rest were pinned down with no available exit. Suddenly she saw the man on the other end of the firearm. He was rushing down the ramp in an attempt to escape to the next level. She and Barnes took off on foot after him. Police back-up, Officer Andrews, arrived and pinned the shooter between him and Barnes. Sgt. Morris ordered him to drop his weapon. Ten minutes later the shooter was handcuffed and sitting in the back seat of Andrews' patrol car.

At the police station, the dumpster diver and the shooter, as well as Fitz were interrogated. Dumpster diver, uncooperative at first, was identified as Mark Sanderson, brother of Melony Sanderson.

"Why were you shooting at the police officers?" asked Detective Roskam.

Sanderson stared at the detective. Angrily he responded, "I only wanted Rodriguez!"

"Why?"

"He arrested my sister and now she's in prison for life. I will get him if it's the last thing I do!" Sanderson curtly responded.

Mark Sanderson was then placed in a different room under police guard. The detectives immediately recognized this as a crime of vengeance, as Melony was the one who murdered the chief's brother, Willy.

Now it was the second shooter's time with the detectives. He identified himself as Donald Sanderson, brother of Mark and Melony, and he wasn't talking. "I got nothing to say to you!"

The police then went to Fitz. Fitz wasn't under arrest but was taken to the police station by Sgt. Morris.

"What were you doing in the parking garage tonight?" asked Detective Roskam.

"I was following someone. Trying to get a positive ID for my client," Fitz responded.

"And who is your client?" demanded Detective Roskam.

"Look. I am a private investigator. Mrs. Helen Sanderson hired me to find her son, Donald," replied Fitz. "I was supposed to give him this envelope." Fitz pulled a sealed envelope from his coat pocket.

"And what's in the envelope?" asked Detective Roskam.

"I have no idea," responded Fitz.

"Give it to me then. Let's see what's in it," demanded Roskam. He opened the envelope only to find a handwritten note. He read it. "Seems like Mom Sanderson was aware that her son Mark was out to murder one of our own. Seems like she was trying to find Donald, her other son, to warn him that his brother Mark was armed and willing to shoot anyone to get revenge for Melony. Seems like Donald has been on Mark's trail for a while and hasn't been in touch with his mother. The note is a warning to Donald to stay away and avoid taking any steps to prevent Mark from doing anything. Note says *don't get yourself killed*. This is a police matter. Why are you in the middle of this, Fitz?"

"Like I said. I was only hired to identify this man and give him the note. I don't know anything else," responded Fitz.

Right then, Sgt. Morris entered the interrogation room, handed Detective Roskam a note, and then left the room. The note read: *It turns out that Donald Sanderson has no police record. Mark Sanderson is on supervised parole for armed robbery.* Detective Roskam then understood why Mrs. Sanderson did not involve the police. She knew her son, Mark, was not allowed to possess a firearm while on parole, so she hired a private investigator to warn her other son to stay away. She figured Mark would get arrested before he could do any real damage to Officer Rodriguez. She did not want two sons in jail.

That evening, Mrs. Sanderson was arrested and brought into the interrogation room as well. Her story checked out exactly the way Detective Roskam had it figured based on the evidence.

At the close of the interrogation process, Detective Roskam was heard to say, "Looks like a dreadful day for the Sanderson family. Three in jail! Now for you, Fitz," said Detective Roskam. "I have nothing to hold you on, so I will let you go. You will be summoned as a witness when the trials start. In the meantime, leave your firearm at home and stick to things you are more qualified for. In the future, make sure you have all the facts before you accept a job. Got it?" Detective Roskam asked condescendingly.

Upon Fitz's release, Sgt. Morris took the opportunity to find out why he had lied to the lieutenant in her favor.

"I know the procedure. I figured you weren't on duty in the Ace of Clubs that night, so you failed to inform me to register at the police station. I didn't want to get you in a jam, so I just gave you credit for advising me to do it."

The next couple of weeks proved to be very slow for Sgt. Morris. She was genuinely relieved that all the excitement was over and assuaged that police work had become mundane again. She learned that there was to be a public ceremony for Officer Rodriguez and Barnes, as well as herself, to receive the department's highest honor, the medal of valor. The chief, the mayor, and the governor were to be in attendance. The media broadcasted this over all public communication mediums and ensured everyone in the state knew about this. On the night of the event, many police officers, firefighters, and dignitaries were present for the ceremony. As Sgt. Morris walked across a makeshift stage, she noticed Bo sitting in the fourth row. She tried to maintain a solemn decorum, a propriety worthy of the night, but deep down was happy to see him. As she gazed two rows deeper into the audience, she also caught sight of Stuart.

Oh, no!

<h1 style="text-align:center">5</h1>

<h1 style="text-align:center">Coping With Doubts</h1>

The following morning, Serena began her shift. She was in a good mood as she spent two hours talking on the phone with Stuart. She was relieved with how things turned out yesterday at the ceremony. She was able to talk with Bo only for a short time before the chief grabbed her for pictures. She saw Stuart cross her path and thanked him when he mouthed congratulations to her, but Stuart was in a hurry and mouthed he would call her later that evening. She motioned a thumbs up sign and continued on her way to pictures.

Enjoying a busy but easy shift, she stopped at the Dine and Dash for lunch. She was used to everyone staring at her while in uniform and maintained a sense of friendliness as she greeted those she walked by in the restaurant. She sat down at a corner booth and waited to be served.

The waitress brought her a menu, and as Serena glanced up, Fitz sat himself down at her table. "Hello, Serena."

"Hi, Fitz. What brings you here?" asked Serena.

"Everybody needs to eat," Fitz responded. "So, what's new with the Sanderson case?"

"You know I can't discuss police business with you," Serena replied. An awkward silence followed.

Finally, Fitz spoke up. "Well, okay, how about we do not discuss our professional lives. Would you join me for dinner tonight?"

"Now why would I do that when you've already joined me for lunch?"

"Uhm. Well, it might be fun to..."

Serena interrupted. "Fun to what? To date? Probably not a good idea. I have to get back on duty now."

"Okay, Serena. Maybe another time." At that, Fitz stood up and walked away.

As Serena watched Fitz walk away, she thought to herself, *that's odd. What does he want with me? What's his end game? Why is he always showing up?*

Serena wouldn't get an answer to that today. Her afternoon took a turn for the worse as she helped to alleviate traffic issues caused by a three-car collision at an intersection. By the time this was cleared, it was time for her to clock out for the day.

On her drive home, Serena immersed herself in some serious reflection. It suddenly dawned on her for the first time just how much danger Rodriguez had been in the night the Sanderson clan was arrested. She thought about the bravery he and Barnes displayed that day and how neither lost their composure. She relived that distinct feeling of euphoria and adrenaline when she intentionally rammed her car into the steel dumpster, which effectively saved the lives of everyone involved.

During her reflective thinking, she caught herself rethinking the profession she had chosen and whether she wanted to continue being a cop. The entire thought process scared her as she had never doubted before. She had wanted to be a policewoman since she was twelve years old, when she saw two policemen arrest a man causing problems in her neighborhood. She recalled how strong they were and how each officer knew exactly what to do. She remembered one of the policemen winking at her as they passed by with the "bad man" in custody. This was the reason she became a cop—to protect good people from bad people. She decided the best thing to do was to talk to Rodrigez and Barnes tomorrow, to see how they were coping. To her own admittedly selfish way of thinking, this inquiry would at the very least allow her the opportunity to connect with her staff, which ultimately may help her to cope with her own feelings.

Tomorrow came and she learned that Rodrigez was terrified that he was the target of a murder plot. He admitted to experiencing nightmares and to losing sleep, and he too was doubting his career choice. He didn't know to whom he could talk, as he did not want anyone to conclude they could not depend on him. He struggled to relate this to Sgt. Morris but did feel better once he released it.

Sgt. Morris learned from Officer Barnes that the day in question was the day she knew she had chosen the right profession and was also the day she had matured quickest. *One tough cookie*, thought Sgt. Morris.

Sgt. Morris set up mandatory counseling for Rodriguez with the police psychologist, a confidential service offered at the Department's expense for such occasions. Sgt. Morris also received these services for her own peace of mind.

The following weekend, Serena and Stuart once again decided to see each other. Stuart drove the two-hour trip to Serena's house. Serena was fearful to leave the house because she worried that she may run into Bo. Since neither Bo nor Stuart knew about each other, and since dating two men at once was a first for Serena, she insisted on staying at home when Stuart arrived.

They talked for hours when Stuart dropped a bomb, "So, are you seeing anyone else?"

Serena thought for a moment about how to respond. Finally, she said, "Well, yes, sort of. I am seeing someone casually every now and again. How about you?"

"I suppose I am. Occasionally I see this waitress at a restaurant that I make a point to frequent. She and I have been discussing going on a date, but so far, we haven't. I think she may be seeing someone, but I'm not sure."

"Oh," responded Serena, "maybe her schedule and yours just don't match right now."

Serena could have slapped herself at that moment. *Why am I making excuses for this woman? They don't need my help. In fact, I wish…* She stopped herself there. *I have no right to claim him for myself. He can date whomever he wants.*

"Let me ask you something," Stuart interjected. "How do you see this relationship? On what path do you see us?"

"Hmm. I was going to ask you the same thing," Serena responded only because she was caught off guard.

"Okay," said Stuart. "I'll go first. I like the fact that you are independent. I love that you enjoy a career and are satisfied with it. I want you to enjoy whatever career you choose for as long as you want. I would never step in and ask you to give it up. There are so many things I appreciate about you. Maybe this is too soon, but we're not teenagers. I cannot stop thinking about you when you are away. I enjoy your company and am thankful we were set up to meet. I am comfortable with seeing only you, but I feel it's a bit too soon to ask of you the same."

"I am at a loss for words right now. I've been seeing this guy for a couple of months. He is completely the opposite of you. I mean, you are tall and strong, outdoorsy, and decisive. Bo is short, but sweet, indecisive, or at least he was, and enjoys trying new things. Dates with him are, oh what is the word, experimental. He likes to try new things like ballet, or opera, or goofy golfing… nothing exactly romantic until the last time we went out, when I saw a romantic side of him. With you, Stuart, I get honesty and openness, subtle romance from the start, decisiveness, and I feel safe." Serena breathed a heavy sigh.

"Okay. It seems you're undecided. May I continue to see you until you decide?" asked Stuart confidently.

"Of course."

"Does he know about me?" asked Stuart.

"No. Look, I have never dated two guys simultaneously. I've been nervous and anxious about it. I will tell him next time I see him."

Serena couldn't help but feel that she ruined the mood and the night. She felt as though she put a damper on things, sort of forcing the date into a corner and choking it out.

Although Stuart tried his best to enjoy the evening, Serena could tell that he was devastated. But she didn't know how to fix it. She thought of how she could better have broached the subject with Stuart. Perhaps she could have been a bit more subtle when deciding to tell Stuart about Bo. She realized she had hurt him.

Stuart, in turn, cut the night short when he informed Serena he had an early day tomorrow and needed to get back home. The reality was that he was going in late tomorrow, which is the reason he wanted to spend a late evening with Serena. Truth be told, he wanted Serena to be his girlfriend exclusively. He had planned out the details to the letter of how he would approach Serena. But none of it mattered. None of it made a bit of difference. He had hoped Serena would yell, "Yes, yes, yes!" when he made his big speech. Instead, he was told, "I will tell my other boyfriend about you." He kissed Serena goodnight and closed the door behind him. He mulled over the events of the evening. He wondered if it was just too soon to ask for a commitment. It was a long, lonely drive back home to Boston.

6

Sergeant Needs Assistance

"Officer needs a supervisor on scene," blared across the police radio.

Sgt. Morris responded she would be on scene in one minute. When she arrived, she observed Officer Helmsley standing with an individual in handcuffs.

"Whatchya got?" asked Sgt. Morris.

"Pulled him over for suspected DWI," replied Helmsley. "He is refusing a breathalyzer and any field sobriety tests."

Sgt. Morris looked at this individual and said, "Sir, I am Sgt. Morris of the Brisbon P.D. If you refuse a breathalyzer, I will have no choice but to arrest you and take you to jail. Are you willing to submit?"

"I refuse my right to pee in public," slurred the inebriated man. "I at least deserve a lieutenant instead of a woman sergeant," he slurred again.

"Go ahead and bring him in, Helmsley," said Morris.

The remainder of the shift, Sgt. Morris found herself focused on both Bo and Stuart. Running through her mind was one simple question: What am I looking for at this stage in my life?

"Officer needs assistance, 5th and Main at Casey's bar."

Sgt. Morris sped to the bar where she was met on scene by Officer Rodriguez. Immediately after Officer Barnes rolled up, coming out of the bar with a combatant individual was Officer Helmsley. He told Sgt. Morris there was a fight inside the bar and one individual still needed to be removed. Sgt Morris took custody of the first combatant and a few minutes later Officer Helmsley and Barnes exited the establishment with the second combatant.

Finally, the end of the shift arrived, and the entire shift was relieved to be done. Sgt. Morris rushed home and began to get ready for her date tonight, with Bo. She was understandably nervous since tonight she would ask the tough questions to Bo. *Just a matter of knowing how to go about it*, she thought.

Bo and Serena took a walk in the park.

Serena took up the cause almost immediately. "Bo, can I ask you something serious?"

"What's on your mind, Serena?" he asked.

"Where is this relationship going? Are we dating with a goal in mind? Are we just having fun?" asked Serena.

At that point they were approaching a park bench. They sat down and awaiting an answer, Serena looked directly in Bo's eyes.

"Well, from my perspective, I'm in no hurry to get serious. I mean, when the time comes and it's right for both of us, no matter who it is, then I will consider getting serious. Until then, I would like to continue to get to know you and just have fun in the process. I mean, I don't know if you're the one. It's too soon for me." A brief pause. "And you?"

"What does serious look like to you? Marriage? Living together. What?" asked Serena.

"Well, I don't know. I've never considered marriage. Living together may be an option. Maybe a long engagement. I think for now it just means making a commitment. Maybe kids someday, as long as their mother is willing to be a stay-at-home mom," responded Bo.

At that point, they continued walking.

During the silent moments of the walk, Serena found herself preoccupied with Bo's response to her questions. She realized he never pursued answers to his questions, which caused her to wonder if he just didn't care or didn't wish to pursue it further. She made a list in her head of the pros and cons of his answers. For starters, not having to commit to anything or anyone certainly left things loose and free. In a way this sounded great as there was no one but self to answer to. On the other hand, that's what Serena has now and it's not so good. A long engagement sounds okay, kids down the road sounds great, but a stay-at-home mom! That wouldn't work for Serena. She was elated at this thought because she finally confirmed that being a cop was what she was meant to be. The doubts she had earlier dissipated. The counseling helped, and tonight's conversation with Bo solidified her career choice.

Her thoughts then changed to Stuart. *Here is a man who knows what he wants and is ready to pursue it soon. Is this what I want? This is also a man who will not try to stifle my career. This is a guy who makes me feel safe, protected. Am I ready to settle down should he ask me in the next year or so?* Self-doubt ran rampant in her mind. *This is a time I need assistance rather than giving assistance!*

Bo and Serena came to the end of their walk. Serena had drifted so far away from the conversation that Bo realized she may not have liked his answers. He reasoned that at least he was honest. *Besides,* he thought, *I'm not that invested in this relationship that I should be considering marriage at this point. I mean, what is the hurry? One day I might.*

The next morning before Serena's shift began, she drove to the cemetery to visit Willy's gravesite.

She placed a flower on his headstone and began talking to him. "Hi, Willy. I love you and miss you, but I need your help. What should I do? I know it's okay with you for me to pursue my life, to love another man, but I am contemplating what is best for me at this stage in my life. I need answers. I need sound advice. I depended on you to help me. I knew you were the one for me, but you were taken from me." She recognized her thoughts wandered, thereby leaving her speech in disarray. "Thank you, Willy, for listening. Thank you for showing me what love means."

As she left the cemetery, tears streamed down her face.

Suddenly, an elderly man arrived and asked her, "Have you lost someone recently?"

"Yes," replied Serena, "my boyfriend, soon to have been my fiancé."

"Oh. I am so sorry. I lost the love of my life six months ago. We had been married forty-eight years and suddenly, with hardly any notice, she was gone. "

"Oh, no. How are you doing?"

"Well, it's hard, but I am learning to accept it and to cope. I'm fortunate to still have our friends who are helping me when I need it," said the elderly gentleman. "How are you doing?"

"Well, I am through grieving, but I am now facing the dilemma of choosing between two men. They both have very fine qualities but are as different as day is from night. I came to talk to my Willy to get some clarity."

"I see," said the elderly man. "Can I give you some advice?"

Serena shook her head yes.

"Don't pick someone you know you can live with. Pick someone you cannot live without."

"Thank you, sir. I will keep that in mind." Serena walked away, understanding that other people have had hurt and pain in their lives as well. She couldn't imagine the pain of losing someone after forty-eight years.

The next few weeks Serena found herself focusing intently on work when at work and on her personal life when not at work. She was feeling better by now and had a clear head. She knew what she had to do and was determined to get it done. First stop—Bo. Second stop—Stuart. During these few weeks she did not see either of them but rather spoke on the phone or texted each of them as much as possible. It was now time to meet with Bo. The two of them agreed to have a short date at a restaurant where Serena expressed her feelings and shared her decision with Bo. The night ended early, as expected.

Serena, arriving back home, immediately phoned Stuart and asked to see him. They agreed to meet at a local restaurant about one hour from each of them on Friday night.

On the drive to the restaurant, Serena began to get nervous. She was happy that she decided to talk to Stuart in person, concluding that a personal touch was not only necessary but the right thing to do. She felt the same way in conversing with Bo.

As she pulled into the restaurant parking lot, she noticed Stuart waiting by the entrance door with a bouquet of roses in hand. She ran a quick comb through her hair, checked her makeup, and sprayed a little perfume on her wrists and rubbed them together. *I guess Stuart deserves my best since I did my best for Bo as well*, she thought.

Serena took a deep breath and stepped out of her car. She slowly made her way to the entrance door.

Stuart stood awaiting Serena and hugged her. He had no idea what was coming, but he did manage to assume the best. *It's got to be me!* he thought. *It's just got to!*

7

Cool as a Cucumber

"Thank you for the beautiful roses, Stuart," Serena said. "They are absolutely gorgeous!"

"You're welcome," responded Stuart. "They reminded me of you."

The two of them sat down at a table, ordered their food, and engaged in small talk.

Finally, Serena began a more serious conversation; the reason she came here. "Stuart, remember what you asked me a while back, you know, making a decision between you and Bo."

"Yes, I remember."

"Well, I reached a decision."

Just then, the waitress appeared with their orders. Serena looked at Stuart who seemed to be understandably nervous.

"I have spoken with Bo and worked through what he is wanting in a relationship. He is a great guy whom I have grown fond of and learned his goals and life plan, at least for now. I have chosen a path that suits me better, that is, if you will still have me," Serena smiled. A short pause ensued, and Serena continued, "I would like to take you up on your offer that we see only each other."

Stuart let out a big sigh, the kind a person would let out after a charging bear suddenly changed directions and ran away. "I was hoping you would say that, Serena. There is only one thing."

Serena's smile jumped off her face. "You decided to date that waitress?"

"No, no. This business of seeing you only once or twice a month needs to change. I very much intend to find ways we can spend more time together, that is, if you'll have me," Stuart stated very reassuringly.

Stuart grabbed Serena's hand from across the table. They both leaned toward the center of the table and shared a kiss. Serena's heart was racing. She felt like a giddy schoolgirl on a first date. Stuart's eyes beamed with excitement as the two of them raced to set times they would see each other. Serena agreed to spend more weekends at her parents' house, closer to Stuart, and Stuart suggested he could drive to Brisbon maybe twice per month, and both could drive an equal distance to see each other as well, like they did tonight.

Just then, a scream was heard at the front of the restaurant. A young teenager claiming he had a gun in his pocket demanded the money from the waitress at the cash register. Serena instructed Stuart to call the local police and advise them of what was happening and that there was a plainclothes female police sergeant from Brisbon on scene. Serena then ducked behind the tables as she made her way closer to the teenager. When she managed to get within ten feet of the boy, she grabbed a pan-style pizza from a table and stayed low.

When she was five feet away, she screamed, "Hey, pizza face!"

The boy turned around quickly, only to be slammed in the face with the steaming hot pan pizza. Serena hair snatched the teen to the floor and reached for her hand cuffs inside her jacket pocket. She was about to put them on the teen's wrists when the local police arrived on scene. Serena identified herself with badge and ID while the local authorities removed the teen from the restaurant and placed him in the back seat of the squad car. The police then gathered the written statements from all those involved and from all witnesses and left the scene.

As the restaurant patrons broke out in applause for Serena's quick thinking, she calmly sat down back at the table with Stuart and very quietly said, "Now where were we?"

"That was amazing!" exclaimed Stuart. "How in the world did you come up with a pizza to the face plan so quickly?"

"It's my job. It's kind of what I do. This was a punk kid whom I doubt even had a gun in his pocket. All he wanted was some beer and cigarette money, most likely. Maybe some gas money," Serena responded.

"Wow! You move like a tigress in a concrete jungle. So sleek, so quiet, and smooth! And when you pounce, you don't mess around!"

"Yes, Stuart. Deep dish pizzas are the only way to fly," Serena said laughingly.

The next workday Serena was summoned into the chief's office. There she was told that the jury had been selected and the trial for Mark, Donald, and Ma Sanderson was about to start. On Thursday, the A.G. would be questioning Sgt. Morris and the other officers involved. He said it should be pretty routine but cautioned her to read all the reports submitted just to refresh her memory and remind her officers to do the same. The chief was correct. Thursday came and the testimony of Sgt. Morris, Officer Helmsley, Officer Barnes, and Officer Rodriguez was heard. Detective Roskam also gave his testimony. Body camera footage was submitted as evidence as well as pictures of the scene of the crime. Fitz gave his testimony as to his role in the unfolding incident. The attorney for the defense was frustrated by the A.G. because he would not agree to a plea deal. In the end, Mark Sanderson was committed to life in prison; Donald Sanderson received a fifteen-year sentence, and Helen Sanderson received a light sentence of one year suspended to parole for three years.

As the sentences for each were given, Sgt. Morris noticed something strange when Helen was given her sentence. She looked directly at Fitz and smirked. Fitz nodded his head and then watched Helen walk away, escorted by a department of corrections employee and a deputy sheriff. The somber look on Fitz's face as she walked away made Sgt. Morris tense and caused the hair on the back of her neck to rise. A cold chill ran eerily down the length of her spine and then back up. Fitz then made eye contact with Sgt. Morris. Sgt. Morris turned away from his gaze and proceeded out of the courtroom.

As she resumed her duties in her patrol car, she decided to drive to the parking garage once again. She observed that the steel dumpster she purposely crashed was removed and wasn't replaced. The space that it previously had occupied looked cold and empty, sort of like the expression on Fitz's face only twenty minutes ago. She exited her patrol car and walked the area, remembering every detail of the incident. She was haunted by the interaction between Fitz and Helen at sentencing and wondered what she had missed.

Getting back into her squad car, she reviewed in her mind every interaction she had had with Fitz, starting with the Ace of Clubs bar and restaurant, the time Fitz had asked her on a date, and ending with the cold, empty look he had sent her way after sentencing. *Something is off*, she thought. *What did I miss?*

About that time, Rodriguez drove up in his patrol car. The two of them talked through rolled down windows.

"I see you have the same thought I have."

"I do," replied Sgt. Morris. "I thought I'd take another look around. Did you notice the dumpster is gone?"

"Yea. It was moved a few weeks ago," responded Rodriguez.

"Oh. Have you been here since I crashed it?"

"Yes," responded Rodriguez. Been here a couple of times since then. Was just trying to get some clarity. Police psychologist suggested it may help, as long as I don't dwell on it. Feels good to be done with it, you know Sarge?"

"Yes, it does," replied a skeptical Serena. "Yes, it does."

8
Revelation

"**F**inally," Serena said to herself, "date night."

It was Friday night and Serena was once again driving north to see her parents, but more importantly, to see Stuart. The plan was for Stuart to pick Serena up at her parents and take her dancing. 7:00 and the doorbell rang.

"Right on time," Serena said to her parents as she headed to answer the door. "Hi, Stuart, so good to see you."

"Hi, Serena. Wow! You look amazing," Stuart said excitedly.

Serena was wearing a shorter skirt and high heels. She had curled her hair and applied makeup, apparently just the way Stuart liked it. *Well, this is going better than expected*, Serena thought.

"I thought we'd head over to The Blue Lagoon for drinks and dancing. Hopefully you won't have to throw a pizza at anyone tonight!" Stuart said jokingly.

Serena just smiled and said, "Let's hope not. I'm not exactly dressed for brawling."

On the dance floor, Stuart admitted he's not much of a dancer. He told Serena that he was hoping she could teach him to dance, but no luck as Serena was a beginner as well. They were clumsy together, at best, but laughed and smiled with each other every time they took to the floor. The only time they maintained a semblance of dancing was during slow dances, when Stuart enjoyed holding Serena in his arms, and Serena draped her arms over Stuart's neck and shoulders. They seemed to move to the music as one, a single unit, a time for stealing a few kisses and pressing against one another in a romantic display of affection. It was also a night for getting to know each other, a night of communicating at a deeper level, a night that Serena needed after a rough week at work. For Stuart, it was a night to bond with a gorgeous woman and to create an environment of happiness and easiness for Serena. He understood she had a tough job, and he wanted to take her mind off work at least for one night.

Part of the joy Stuart also pocketed from the night was the opportunity to share his work with Serena. He was happy to explain to her in great detail what a wildlife biologist does. He was currently involved in obtaining accurate counts of the whitetail deer in Massachusetts and identifying from these counts the number of deer suffering from CWD, chronic wasting disease. He enjoyed his time in the forest and his interaction with hunters and farmers who brought in dead deer exhibiting CWD. It made his job easier to analyze these deer by county, by age, and by percentage of confirmed CWD in any given area.

Serena found his work very interesting and asked relevant questions, especially when he drove her back to her parents' place. She told Stuart she was happy he enjoyed his work and that his line of work was probably something she may have enjoyed had she been involved in studying that in college. Stuart was thankful she was interested in his work and listened to him as well as she did. It was 1 a.m. when Stuart ended the date, and with a kiss at the door, told Serena he would pick her up at noon for lunch and a walk in the forest.

The entire weekend was an eye-opener for both Stuart and Serena. Serena commented to herself at the end of the weekend that she made the correct decision in releasing Bo and laying claim to Stuart.

She concluded that Stuart had a personality more like her own and a love of the outdoors that she wanted as well. Stuart enjoyed the simple things in life. He was happy to walk in the forest, throw rocks from the shore into a lake, watch a movie at home, and enjoy a picnic in a meadow. *And he's definitely got the better build!*

Stuart did not come away with any new revelations about Serena. He knew what he wanted from the start and made his play for her early on. He knew she was a strong, independent woman, and this was solidified in his mind when he watched Serena hair-snatch pizza face. *Exactly the woman I have waited for: bravado in one moment and all woman the next!*

When the weekend came to a joyous close, Serena's mother Rhoda began a conversation with Serena.

"So, honey, you've been seeing Stuart for a while now."

"Yes, Mom, I have."

"Is it serious, dear?" asked an inquisitive mother. "I mean, what can I tell your father when he gets back home?"

"I suppose you can tell him that you and he raised an intelligent daughter who knows how to choose a wonderful man. You can tell him that I like Stuart, and that Stuart is a good man who doesn't try to control me, nor is he threatened by my job. You can tell Dad that as we learn more about each other, we understand more and more what we are looking for in a partner."

"All good, honey. But do you love him?" asked Rhoda.

"Not sure, Mom. I can tell you that I am having a difficult time knowing I have to go back to Brisbon without him."

"Okay dear, it sounds to me like you are falling in love. We like Stuart as well and are very happy for you," replied Rhoda.

"Thanks, Mom. I suppose I better hit the road. Got a two-hour drive ahead of me and am meeting Stuart for a quick ice cream cone in about ten minutes. Tell Daddy I love him, and I love you too." With that, Serena headed out the door and drove to the Ice Cream Haus.

On her drive home, she couldn't help but shed some tears as it was difficult for her to say goodbye to Stuart after such a wonderful weekend. She recalled the picnic in the middle of the forest. She chuckled at how silly Stuart became as he skipped flat stones into Lake Linda. She experienced chills as she recalled how Stuart held her and kissed her during the weekend activities. She couldn't wait for next weekend when Stuart would drive to Brisbon. She also caught herself pondering the question her mother asked her before she left: D*o I love him?*

The week of police work after her glorious weekend offered nothing new or exciting. She went to court on a few traffic citations she had issued weeks before. Traffic accidents, road rage complaints, and even a jaywalker which she ignored were the highlights of her week. In the back of her mind, she was counting the days until she would see Stuart again. On one occasion she recalled the advice given by the old man at the cemetery: "Don't pick the one you can live with; rather, choose the one you can't live without."

"I think I do love him," Serena said to herself.

Friday after work came early for both Stuart and Serena. Serena had prepared the guest bedroom in her house for Stuart to stay in during the weekend. Serena found herself daydreaming that she told Stuart she loved him, and that Stuart returned the sentiment. She realized she was acting like a high school girl with a crush on someone, but also realized her feelings were much deeper than that. She wondered if she should be the first to say those three words, or should she wait for Stuart to utter those words first. She was excited at the prospect of Stuart saying I love you, but at the same time realized Stuart may not feel the same yet or may not be ready to say it yet.

Stuart arrived early Friday evening. Serena met him in her driveway and offered to help him carry any luggage he may have brought into her house.

"No, Serena, I am in a motel just off the interstate. I respect you too much to even give you the impression that I am here to take advantage of you. I want your parents to know just what kind of a person I am."

"Oh. Okay," responded an excited Serena. "Well, come in. I have a weekend planned for us."

As they walked into her house, Serena couldn't help but smile at how much of a gentleman Stuart was, and how much she respected his view on their relationship. *I'm definitely going to tell him how I feel sometime this weekend*, she thought.

Friday night was a slow night. A movie at home on the television, followed by a brisk walk outside. Saturday a drive to a county forest, lunch at a local restaurant, an afternoon of biking, and then the highlight of the evening, miniature golf! Stuart laughed that Serena considered goofy golfing the highlight, but in the same breath was thankful as the fifteen-mile bike ride had worn him out. Serena, who had been running her four miles a day route since before her promotion to sergeant, had no problem with the bike ride and was ready for more. She was struggling with her timing to engage in a more serious conversation. Every time she attempted to engage, her thoughts interfered with her words.

Suddenly, Stuart spoke up. "Nice putt, Serena. Let me ask you something. How many children do you see us having after we're married?"

"Uhm, what?" asked Serena. "Excuse me!"

"Pretty simple question, really," Stuart said jokingly. "You know, rugrats. How many do you want?"

They moved aside and let the family behind them move ahead to continue their golf game. "Stuart, we haven't even said I love you…"

Stuart interrupted her before she could complete her sentence. "I love you too."

Serena ran to Stuart's now open arms. "Of course, I will marry you."

"I haven't proposed yet," Stuart said.

"Two children. A boy and a girl. But not right away."

Stuart dropped to one knee and fearlessly showed Serena her engagement ring.

Serena, awestruck, looked at it, and keeping in the spirit of the backwardness of the situation, asked Stuart, "Will you marry me?"

Stuart by now was laughing so hard he could hardly balance any longer on one knee. When he was able to speak again, he said, "Well, your dad already said yes, and I know your mom grilled you with questions last weekend! So, I guess my answer is yes. Now, are YOU wearing this ring, or am I?"

Serena held out her ring finger, and before Stuart placed it on her finger, he very politely asked, "Serena, I love you. Will you do me the honor of becoming my wife?"

"Of course, I will. I love you too."

Stuart slid the ring on her finger. Serena held it up to the light and marveled how it sparkled. Stu noticed a tear running down her cheek which caused his eyes to well up, which of course, he immediately attributed to sinus problems.

Serena, however, knew better and was touched at how sensitive this big strong masculine man had become in the moment.

9
Run For Your Life

As Serena drove in to work the next day, she heard the news on the local radio station.

"KBBX news, your station with explanation. Shocking news coming from the Brisbon Police Department. The wife of Chief Larry Breckenridge caught in an affair with another man. Details at eight. And now, back to the morning show, with Jeff and Dean, your lean and mean music guys."

Oh, no, Serena thought, *how is the chief going to deal with this? Does he know?* She entered the precinct and looked around for the chief. She noticed his door was closed and his secretary outside his office typing something.

"Melony…" she whispered.

"I know. We all know. Chief is not coming in today. Nobody is saying anything. I've already pushed the media out once today. No telling when they'll be back," Melony responded.

"Is it true? Do we know who it is?" asked Serena.

"The media mentioned some Fitz guy, but it's all rumor."

"Fitz? Oh, shit! Sorry Melony, didn't mean to cuss."

"I've heard worse around here, especially from the chief!" responded Melony.

"I've got to find him," said a panicky Sgt. Morris.

"You know him?" asked Melony.

"Yes. I have had several interactions with him, if it's the same guy," Serena replied.

Serena drove Code 3, lights and siren, to the chief's house. She understood that Chief was more than likely to be focused on finding Fitz, so she was hoping to find Sue Ann, the chief's wife, at home. To her relief, the chief's unmarked patrol car was not to be found on his property. Serena knocked on the house door and let herself in.

"Sue Ann," she shouted, "this is Sgt. Morris. Are you here?"

"Hi Serena," said a sullen Sue Ann as she suddenly appeared in the kitchen. "I'm in the bedroom packing."

"What happened?" she asked anxiously.

"Well, I am ashamed to say that I have been having an affair with another man," explained Sue Ann.

"Why? Who?" asked Serena.

"Well, he's a private detective. I met him at a bar, next thing I know we're in a hotel. He's just a guy who was right there at the right time when I needed someone. He's out of my life now. It was a one-time fling."

"What about Larry?" asked Serena.

"You know him, Serena. He's always busy. At meetings, at court, at seminars, at lectures. It was like I didn't exist anymore. So, I did a stupid thing looking for love outside of my marriage," Sue Ann explained.

"Does Larry know?" Serena inquired.

"Does he know? He's furious. You just missed him. I admitted my affair and told him who the other man is, or was, and he peeled out of here like a… well, fast."

"Was it a man named Fitz?" Serena asked.

"Yes. I see you heard it on the news too."

"Is this the same Fitz…"

Sue Ann interrupted. "Yes, it's the same one. Grant Fitzgerald."

"Do you know where he lives?" asked Serena.

"No, but I'm sure Larry does. There was enough paperwork generated from a few months ago to find his address. I called Fitz as soon as Larry peeled out of here. I told him to run, to hide, to get out of town as Larry is furious. Serena, I'm afraid. No telling what Larry will do if he gets his hands on Fitz."

"So, you have his phone number? Give it to me, now!" Serena demanded.

Phone number in hand, Serena sped out of the chief's driveway as fast as she could. She made a call to Fitz's number but found it was no longer in service. After calming down a bit, she decided to call the chief. No answer, so she left a message.

"Chief, this is Serena. Don't do it. It's not worth it. Call me. Let's talk."

No sooner did Serena leave that message than her phone rang. It was the chief.

"Sgt. Morris, this is none of your concern. Your job is to supervise your officers and patrol the streets to keep them safe." He was stern and very angry sounding.

"That's exactly what I'm doing, Chief. Protecting the streets, and that includes Fitz. What he did is low, but no crime was committed!" she exclaimed.

At that, the chief hung up the phone.

"Oh Chief," Serena said to herself, "you're heading down a dangerous path. This will get you fired and put in prison. Come on, Chief, figure it out!"

The rest of the day, Serena struggled with putting out an APB on the chief. She realized that broadcasting an all-persons bulletin was political suicide. That would alert the entire police department to look for the chief, which in turn would definitely leak to the media and embarrass the chief even further. She would not survive such a decision, nor would any officer who found him, not to mention the rumor mill it would facilitate. So, she continued on her own to find the chief or Fitz. Two hours into the next shift, Serena decided to call it a day and go home. When she arrived at her house, in the driveway she saw the chief's cruiser and the chief in the front seat.

"I don't want to talk about this, Sergeant. But after careful consideration of what you said I am suspending my search for Fitz."

"Good, Chief, that's the right decision," Serena said reassuringly.

"Okay, I will see you tomorrow. Good night," and the chief sped away and continued his search for Fitz.

Serena was happy the chief made the right decision but was also sad because she wanted to help him get through this. She wanted to explain that Sue Ann was sorry for what she did and that she realized how big of a mistake her single incident affair really was. Serena desperately wanted to offer support to the chief, but no opportunity was given. All she could hope for now was that the chief would go home and figure out what to do with his marriage. He needed a few days off to work it out with his wife. Nothing more to do tonight, Serena went inside her house somewhat relieved that the chief gave up the chase.

She enjoyed a quick shower, ironed a new uniform for tomorrow, took a brush to her shoes, made dinner, and sat down to enjoy a late dinner. She picked up her phone and called her fiancé. The topic of conversation was one they both were thinking about: a wedding date and where will they live? What about their jobs?

10
Sacrifice Unacceptable

After several weeks, things had fallen into place. The chief hadn't found Fitz and didn't seem to be focused on him anymore. Instead, he spent his time focusing on police work and his wife. Sue Ann had now moved back in with the chief from her mother's house, and rebuilding that relationship became a priority for him.

Serena was wrapped up in her dates and time with Stu, her new nickname for her fiancé. They still had not set a wedding date because they were unable to decide where they would live after the wedding. Stu decided to apply for a job transfer closer to Brisbon; but so far, no offers were given. In fact, both Stu and Serena were saddened by the report that no vacancies existed for a wildlife biologist nearer to Brisbon. The only hope they had was that his application would be kept on file, which was no hope at all.

On this particular evening, Serena and Stu met for dinner with Serena's parents and Stu's mother. The dinner was held at the home of Carl and Rhoda Morris. It was a dinner prepared by both mothers to celebrate the engagement of Stu and Serena, with small undertones of helping the two settle on a wedding date. Stu's mother, Sharon, a widow, was the main motivator in setting the date. Everyone that evening understood the specific problems faced in setting a date, especially as it related to careers and a home. Sharon suggested they both sell their houses and purchase one half-way between. Serena put that to rest immediately when she told everyone of the requirement to live in the city she protects. There was no solution that could be worked out, short of one of them quitting their job and moving. Both opted out of this, saying that wouldn't be fair to either one. By the end of the evening, the only thing confirmed was love. Stu and Serena loved each other. The parents loved the children, and everyone loved the venison dinner.

The next weekend was Stu's turn to drive to Brisbon. He arrived Friday afternoon at Serena's house to an upset Serena.

"I've been calling you all week. Why haven't you answered? Are you okay?" asked a frantic Serena.

"I'm sorry, honey. I've been busy. Come with me. I want to show you something."

They both sat down in Stu's vehicle, even though Serena was still visibly upset, and took a quick drive to the north side of Brisbon. Stu pulled his car into the driveway of a beautiful two-story house. Walking from the house was a realtor, Missy.

Stu introduced the two ladies and explained to Serena that he had been looking at this house and was working hard to find a way to purchase it for the two of them. He said he was willing to give up his career for her after the wedding. The three of them walked through the house as Missy pointed out the features of it, including an impressive backyard. After the tour, Serena could only cry at the sacrifice Stu was willing to make for her, for them. Stu told Missy he would let her know and then drove back to Serena's house.

Serena made it clear to Stu that she was touched by his gesture. She asked him several times if he had thought this decision through thoroughly, and each time Stu responded in the affirmative; but somehow, she knew better. After a long discussion, Stu finally admitted he really did not want to quit his job as he loved what he was doing. He graciously said he would give it all up for her, but Serena was having none of it.

"Look, Stu. Thank you so much. I do love the house, but this is not the way to go about it. We can take more time and figure out a solution. Let's just pass on the house and see what else we can do."

Stu finally came to agree.

She hugged him, gave him a kiss, and they continued to talk.

By the night's end, Stu informed Serena that he would not be able to see her next week. He was heading up north with the game and fish department to engage in continual education both in the lab and in the field. He was leaving Thursday, work straight through the weekend, and come back late Wednesday of the following week. The good news was that he would have a four-day weekend after that, beginning on Thursday.

"I'm all yours for four days," he stated. "What will you do with me?"

Serena laughed. "I'll figure it out. Maybe we could go somewhere. Let me see if I can take that Thursday and Friday off as well," she replied. "Would you be opposed to camping? Oh! Look who I'm asking. You'd live in a tent if you could!"

Stu chuckled.

Stu left her house enroute to a hotel. He plopped down on the bed and fell immediately asleep. Meanwhile, Serena began locking her house doors in preparation for the night's sleep. She heard a knock on the door. When she looked through the peephole after turning on the porch light, she noticed standing at the door was the chief. She let him in and observed that he was drunk.

"Hi, Chief. What have you been up to?"

"Hello there, Sgt. Morris," he slurred. "Can I come in?"

"You are in, Chief!" She chuckled and looked outside. She noticed the chief had driven his own vehicle. "What's going on?" she asked.

"My wife. Sue Ann. She is with Fitz again," the chief slurred.

Serena heard another knock on the door. It was Sue Ann.

She let her in and asked her what this was all about.

"He thinks I'm with Fitz. I was out pretty much all evening with my mom. We were shopping at the mall. When I returned home, he was drunk and accused me of seeing Fitz. I told him he was too drunk to drive. He told me that chiefs of police don't get drunk; at best they get inebriated. I couldn't stop him from driving as he already had the keys, so I jumped in with him. We ended up here."

"I see," Serena said. "Well, I certainly cannot allow him to drive. Do you have keys to your car?"

"Yes, I do." Sue Ann dug through her purse and pulled out a set of keys.

"Okay," replied Serena. "If it's okay with you, let's try to get him to agree to go home with you, as long as you are driving. If not, he can stay in my empty bedroom or the couch until he sleeps it off."

"Sounds good, Serena. And thank you." They turned to find the chief. He was asleep on the couch.

"I guess he'll sleep it off here, Sue Ann," stated Serena.

"Yes, I guess. Do you mind if I spend the night in your extra bedroom?" asked Sue Ann.

"No problem. I'm sure I can round up a pair of pajamas for you. But first, let's take his car keys away from him," Serena replied.

At 6:30 a.m., Serena and Sue Ann woke up and began preparing breakfast. Eggs, bacon, toast, and coffee were on the menu. Around 6:45, the chief woke up. He looked around from his position on the couch and realized he was at Serena's place. He had been there many times before, particularly when she was dating Willy, his brother.

"What smells so good?" asked the chief.

"Bacon and eggs," answered Sue Ann.

"How'd I get here?"

"You drove here," Sue Ann replied.

"When did I get here?"

"Last night," again replied Sue Ann.

"Got anything for a headache?"

"Don't you mean a hangover?" Sue Ann replied.

"Either way. Got anything, Serena?"

"Sure, Chief. Coffee and aspirin," replied Serena. She poured him a cup of coffee and brought the aspirin to his place at the table.

They all sat at the table and began eating. Conversation was non-existent as both women were wondering what the chief remembered from last night.

After minutes of silence, the chief spoke up. "Guess I was a real heel last night."

"You got drunk because you thought I was with Fitz. You knew I was with my mother at the mall," Sue Ann said. She walked to her purse and handed Larry the mall receipts.

"What's this?" asked the chief.

"Receipts. Receipts from the mall last night. Proof that I wasn't with Fitz," Sue Ann said sternly.

"Okay, okay, okay," Larry responded. "I'm sorry. I acted like a jerk! Serena, thank you for the breakfast and letting me stay the night."

"No problem, Chief, and don't worry, our little secret."

Sue Ann and Serena hugged and said goodbye to each other. Serena could feel Sue Ann's appreciation, realizing they may have just avoided a major incident.

11

I Can't Say a Thing

As Larry and Sue Ann drove away from Serena's house, Stu was just arriving.

"Company so early?" asked Stu.

"Yes. The chief and his wife unexpectedly stopped by for a quick visit. We had breakfast and then they left," responded Serena.

"Rough night?"

"Not really. Why do you ask? Serena asked.

"Just the blanket on the couch."

"Oh, that. I woke up early and was a little chilly," Serena lied.

Stu knew something was amiss, but he also understood that sometimes police business need not be pursued. He had accepted the fact that Serena could not discuss much of her job with him.

"Okay, so is there any of that left for me?" Stu asked while pointing at the frying pan.

"Sure is. Eggs, bacon, and toast."

"Just eggs for me. Oh, and coffee," said Stu.

Monday morning came much too quickly for Serena. She had enjoyed the previous day with Stu, and knowing she couldn't see him for ten days made it harder to say goodbye. Their relationship was pressing on both of them to become intimate, but to date they both fought off temptation. They had agreed earlier to wait until they were married, to make the ceremony more relevant and the honeymoon more meaningful. Besides, as Stu mentioned to Serena, it's the way God intended it.

Serena entered the precinct door where Officer Barnes told her that Lieutenant Baker was waiting for her. She entered Baker's office where she was told to close the door behind her.

"Did Chief get home alright Saturday?" he asked.

"Uhm…" Serena stalled.

"Don't worry, Sergeant. I'm in your corner. I observed the chief and his wife driving Friday night. I ran interference for him as he drove to your house. I know he was drunk," Baker stated.

"Well, Lieutenant, he and his wife slept at my place Friday night and went home together Saturday morning. By then he was sober," Sgt. Morris responded.

"We can't let this get out, Sergeant. It's the chiefs reputation. It's the department's reputation."

"Not to worry. I already told him it was our secret."

"If it gets out, I will be looking for you," Baker semi-threatened.

"Right back at you," Sergeant Morris responded.

"Okay, just so we're clear."

"Crystal clear," Sgt. Morris replied.

"Thank you. Sergeant. Have a good shift. Stay safe."

The shift for Sergeant Morris was somewhat lackluster. She and her officers met at various locations as calls for a supervisor were made, but nothing too interesting. Just before the shift's end, however, Sgt. Morris spotted Fitz. He was driving down a one-way street in the mid-town district. She had no cause to pull him over but did so anyway. As she approached his vehicle, Sgt Morris tapped a taillight just hard enough to break it but discreet enough to go unnoticed. When she arrived at Fitz's car window, she asked for the usual documentation from Fitz and explained the reason she stopped him: a broken taillight.

"Come on, Serena, we both know why you stopped me."

"Busted taillight. Here is your citation. You have five days to fix it and show it to the clerk of the county courthouse, at which time the fine will be dropped," answered Sgt. Morris.

Okay, I know the drill. Is it safe to be back in the city?" asked Fitz.

"You mean is the chief still ready to teach you some manners?" asked Sgt. Morris. She wanted to say, "beat the stuffing out of you," but couldn't put the chief or the department in that situation.

"Hey, it just happened. Neither one of us planned it that way. It started out so innocent."

"Yea, right," responded Sgt. Morris. "And then you decided it would be wise to sleep with the police chief's wife. You're not too bright, are you? Creep!"

"I'm a lot smarter than you think," argued Fitz.

"Five days to get your taillight fixed," responded Sgt. Morris and she walked back to her patrol car.

She went home that evening feeling good about sticking up for the chief. She also realized that once the chief found out she had Fitz in her clutches, he wouldn't be happy. He would demand to know why she didn't call him to her location. She reassured herself she did the right thing, as having an affair was not against the law; therefore, the chief had no legal precedence to take any action against Fitz. Larry Fitzgerald, maybe, but not Chief Fitzgerald.

The next morning, she found herself in the chief's office getting grilled. Lt. Baker was called to his office as well. To Sgt. Morris' surprise, he actually sided with her. An angry Chief ordered them both out of his office when he realized the two of them were sticking together.

Tuesday morning brought no surprises to Sgt. Morris, nor did her duties on shift that day. In fact, the rest of the week provided no excitement for Sgt. Morris. When Friday night came, she simply went home. With nothing to do as Stu wasn't an option, she decided to take an early evening jog, followed by a hot shower, and then off to bed. Time passed quickly and before too long it was Saturday morning.

Serena woke up and decided to drive to Fitz's house. She remembered his address from his driver's license the night she pulled him over. She wanted to see where he lived, if for no other reason than to satisfy her curiosity. Upon arrival, she observed the chief's car parked in the parking lot of the apartment complex. She made her way to Apartment #107, and there was the chief, peering through a window.

The chief saw Serena. "This place is empty," he said. "Looks like he moved out."

"This is the address on his DL," Serena replied.

"I know, I found it in the system. That's what your citation read. What are you doing here, Serena?"

"Just curious where this guy has been staying. And you?" asked Serena.

"I came here to kick his ass!"

"Chief, why don't we get some coffee somewhere and talk about it?" Serena suggested. "Let's go to my house."

The chief initially said he would meet Serena at her house. Serena was happy to hear that maybe, just maybe she would be able to get through to the chief; the thing she had been trying to do all along.

About a mile from her house, she looked in her rear view. The chief was gone.

12
No Apology Needed

Unfortunately, the chief had no desire to discuss anything with anyone. He remained headstrong with thoughts solely focused on revenge. No matter what Serena said, even to the point of laying a guilt trip on the chief, she could not get him to settle down or to talk.

Serena drove back home alone, realizing she had done what she could. Once home, she packed an overnight bag, and drove to her parents' home. She desperately wanted to tell her parents what was going on with the chief and maybe get some advice. But she knew she could not divulge police business, especially where the chief is concerned.

The upcoming wedding was the topic for discussion today, as it usually was. Rhoda was a bit disappointed that her daughter and her fiancé had made no more progress since the last time they had talked.

"It seems to me that you both need to get serious about this and figure it out," Rhoda said rationally.

"I know, Mom. We are serious about getting married. We just are struggling with careers and logistics," Serena responded.

"I suppose, dear. Someone has to give in if this wedding is going to happen."

"Mom, let's go into town and do some shopping," Serena suggested, mainly as a way to change the subject.

"Okay, I could use a day of shopping, and your father could use a nap," Rhoda said sarcastically.

While driving around town, Serena and Rhoda both noticed Stuart walking down the sidewalk.

"Look!" shouted Serena, "it's Stuart."

"Yes, I see," said Rhoda, "with another woman!

"Mom, he's supposed to be out-of-town working," Serena said jealously. "He's not supposed to be with her!"

"Should we follow them?" asked Rhoda.

"No, Mom. I prefer to trust him. There must be a good reason he is in town and with that, that woman! He's never given me a reason to doubt him, and I'm not going to start now," Serena stated. "He will call me tonight."

"Okay, dear. I think that is wise."

The rest of the day the two of them became shopping machines. From one store to the next, here and then there, and all the while Serena struggling with trusting Stu. Every time they walked into or past the men's department in any store, thoughts of Stu with that other woman rushed into Serena's head, causing her to doubt and then to put her best foot forward in order to quell it.

Rhoda could see that Serena was preoccupied, and she tried her best to reassure her. She also understood why Serena felt this way, thinking she would feel similar in a similar situation herself. But the shopping went on and the purchasing power of two credit cards was astonishing. If credit cards could talk, both would be complaining about the pain they are feeling every time they were swiped through a credit card machine!

Finally, Rhoda called a truce, saying that she had better stop spending as she is already in trouble with Carl.

"Once he sees these bills, I'm going to hear about it," Rhoda said half-laughingly.

That evening, Stu called Serena. Serena was trying her best not to unveil any emotions, but when Stu asked how she was doing, she wanted to explode.

"Well, I'm visiting my parents."

Stu interrupted. "Oh, I wish I would have known that. We came back to town today to go to my office to pick up some equipment we needed."

"We?" asked Serena.

"Oh, that's right, you don't know her. My supervisor Maggie and I drove back to the office to get some testing equipment. When we were done, I had to hang out at a restaurant while she visited her husband and kids for half an hour. Had I known you were in town, I could have visited with you," Stu explained.

Serena breathed a silent sigh of relief. *Thank goodness*, she thought. *I knew I had nothing to worry about.* She smirked, realizing she didn't fare too well in the trust department. *I better not tell him I saw him today.* It felt good to talk to Stu again. Just to hear his voice, his reassuring voice.

"Maybe after work today, I could drive to your parent's house to see you for a little bit," Stu suggested.

"Or maybe we could meet somewhere so you don't have to drive so far," Serena recommended.

They met at a small-town park about forty-five minutes from both of them. Serena gave Stu a big hug and started to cry.

"What's wrong, babe?" asked Stu.

"It's me. I saw you this afternoon with Maggie, and I thought the worst. I am so sorry. I tried to trust you, but it was so hard. When I saw you walking with her… I'm so sorry, Stu."

"Serena, no need to apologize. I can understand why you would draw that conclusion," Stu said sympathetically. "It's okay. Let's talk about our wedding."

Serena continued to clutch Stu.

As her crying faded, her smiling face peered out from hiding. "You know, honey, we haven't even set a wedding date yet."

"I know," Stu replied. "Isn't that silly? Let's set a date."

"Really?" Serena questioned in disbelief. "You think we can come up with something right now?"

"I know I can. I'm ready. We've waited long enough," Stu replied lovingly. "You pick the month, and I'll pick the day. "

"June. It's October now, so that gives us a little time to work everything out," Serena bubbled.

"Well, that didn't take you long!" Stu replied laughingly. "June it is, and since I don't want to wait until the end of June, I say June 3rd."

"Okay, June 3rd it is." Serena clutched Stu again, but this time for a different reason. "I can hardly wait to become Mrs. Serena Matthews."

"Okay, honey. As much as I would like to see this moment last forever, I have to get back to work. Tomorrow is an early day for me."

"Okay. I understand. June 3rd, right?" asked Serena.

Stu shook his head. "Definitely." He pulled Serena close and kissed her. "No worries, Serena. I loved you from the beginning, and I'll love you through eternity. You never need to worry," Stu stated romantically.

"Thank you, Stu. I feel the same."

Serena left the park with a glide in her stride, a smile on her face, and a glow that could outshine the moon. She couldn't wait to share her wedding date with her parents, especially her mother. *Progress,* she thought. *Progress.*

13
Just Another Day

Monday morning and back to work for Serena. First stop was the chief's office.

"Serena, I have asked you here for a reason. I know how I've been acting lately, and I know how I have been making you feel. I also know that all your decisions have been in my best interest and in the best interest of the department. But I have to tell you that until you have experienced betrayal from a loved one, you have no idea how it much it hurts."

"No, I guess not," replied Serena, "but you still have to function within the realms of reason and within the law. You cannot go off half-cocked, looking to avenge who has wronged you, especially when you are a duly sworn police officer."

"Until I get satisfaction from the man who 'took' my wife, I will not stop. Call it revenge, call it male ego. I have to do this," the chief stated unconditionally.

"Okay, Chief, but know this. As long as I am a sworn peace officer, I will be doing everything by the book and within the law. And that goes for any interference I may have to run on you. I owe that to you." Serena was resolute.

She exited the chief's office and conducted morning briefing with her officers. Little did she know where the day's events would lead her.

The first call led her to a gas station. Officer Barnes was in a physical confrontation with a would-be robber. Sgt. Morris hair-snatched the perpetrator just to find his toupee dangling from her hand. She took out her PR 24, a wooden club she retrieved from a loop on her duty belt and cracked this man on the thighs. The man immediately yelled and writhed in pain as he crawled off Officer Barnes, holding his thigh.

Once in handcuffs and seated in the back seat of the patrol car, this man began screaming, "Police brutality!"

"Shut up!" said Barnes. "You're going to jail!"

"You alright?" Serena asked Barnes.

"Yep, good to go. Just another day. Thanks for your help, Sarge."

"Okay. That's what I'm here for," replied Sgt. Morris calmly. "By the way, I put that man's hair in the front seat of your squad!"

The second call also came from Barnes. Upon arrival, Sgt. Morris observed Barnes engaged with a man and a woman involved in obvious road rage.

"Sarge, can you take this guy away for a few minutes while I get her story?" She pointed toward the woman involved.

The third call came from Officer Helmsley. He found himself in the middle of a food fight at a Chinese buffet. No fist fighting or any real danger at this point, but Helmsley called just to ensure it stayed that way.

"Hey, Sarge. Welcome to the China Palace, home of flying roasted duck and kung pao chicken! High school kids. Jocks against the brainy kids."

"What's your plan, Helmsley?"

He pointed to a few of the brainy kids. "Thought I would toss a few of those dumplings there, especially the red-haired kid, outside which should stop the flying cuisine."

"Okay. Go for it. I've got your back," Sgt Morris laughingly stated.

"Actually, a flying chicken's got my back already!"

The fourth call came from Officer Rodriguez. Sgt. Morris arrived on scene just to find Rodriguez getting ready to handle a domestic violence call.

"Apparently a woman either stabbed or is about to stab some man. I have no idea who this man is or what his relationship is with the woman." He then pointed to a plain clothes man standing next to him. "This is Deputy Sheriff Kirkland of…"

"Hey, Quirky. What are you doing here?"

"I live in these apartments. Just thought I could help."

Looking back at Rodriguez, she asked, "So, what's the plan?"

"I thought we'd listen at the door before we knocked. Then we'll have to assess things from there," Rodriguez replied.

"Okay, Rod. Let's go," said Deputy Sheriff Kirkland.

"Be sure to look through windows as well. See what you can see," said Sgt. Morris.

By now, a small crowd had gathered near the upstairs apartment. Rodriguez knocked.

A door opened and Deputy Sheriff Kirkland yelled, "Knife!"

A woman wielding a knife was holding it between herself and a man across the living room floor. Firearms from all three peace officers were drawn as Rodriguez gave orders to the woman to drop the knife.

"I can't," she cried. "He's going to kill me!"

"Drop the knife now."

The woman dropped the knife and Deputy Sheriff Kirkland pulled the woman by the arm out the door and into the control of Sgt. Morris. By then the man was face down on the floor, legs apart, and arms spread over his head. Rodriguez cuffed him until he could get both sides of the story.

Sgt. Morris' fifth call came from a city bus driver. A fight on the bus between two men. Sgt. Morris called for backup and waited. Officer Barnes arrived, and both of them broke up the fight.

"Thanks for your quick response, Barnes," Sgt. Morris said.

"No problem, Sarge. That's what I'm here for."

By the shift's end, Sgt. Morris was exhausted, Helmsley was full of food, Barnes was happy as could be, and Rodriguez was relieved he made it through the day.

Sgt. Morris offered her praises. "Nice job today, ladies and gentlemen. Nice display of teamwork. Nobody hurt. I would like to say let's all get something to eat, it's on me, but looks like Helmsley's got that covered."

Helmsley rolled his eyes. They all laughed and walked to their cars and drove away.

Sgt. Morris went straight home. She made herself some pizza rolls in the microwave and sat down on the sofa for dinner. *Pizza and a beer!* she thought. *Living large!* By 7:30, she had fallen asleep on the sofa, only to be awakened by her phone. It was Stu.

"Hi, honey. Everything is fine but I can't talk. I'm exhausted from my day from hell. Can we talk tomorrow?"

"Oh, I'm sorry, babe. Real quick, I have good news. I have a chance for a promotion which would bring me back to within fifteen minutes of Brisbon. I take a written exam next week. Highest score gets the offer," Stu explained.

"That's great, honey, I've got to go back to sleep. Good night." And she hung up the phone.

Stu laughed. "Wait for it. Wait for it," he said to the phone.

Suddenly, *Ring!* He answered his phone.

"You what? You have a chance to move closer? Why didn't you tell me? You have to take a test? What kind of a test? For what position? Stu, this is huge! When were you planning on telling me?"

"Uhm, I just did," Stu responded. He could barely talk as he was laughing so hard. "It's a supervisory position. I would still be in the field, but now I would be in charge of a group of biologists. It's at our resources substation in Walker," he responded.

"Walker? That's only fifteen minutes east of Brisbon. Is this something you want?" asked a much calmer Serena.

"Well, the pay is good. The hours are the same. The job is pretty much the same. Yes, I want it," Stu answered.

"Oh, I'm so excited. Can't wait to see you Thursday night!" Serena stated.

14
Wow!

Thursday couldn't come soon enough for Serena. She worked a full shift today but did manage to get Friday off. Stu arrived Thursday afternoon and let himself inside Serena's house. He was excited for his four-day weekend. Finally, at the end of the afternoon, Serena walked through the doorway and ran right into Stu's waiting arms.

"Hi, hi, hi, honey," Serena screamed excitedly. "I missed you so much."

"I missed you as well. So, tell me, how are you?" asked Stu.

Serena began to tear up. "It's been a terribly difficult week for me. First, I see you with another woman and automatically think the worst. Next, my officers and I deal with so much violence on the streets, violence that puts our lives and safety in jeopardy. Then I have to deal with emotional decisions from a superior, who without me could be in jail right now. It never ends!"

"Sounds horrible. I am so sorry. What can you tell me specifically about this? Even if I can't help, it may just be good to vent," Stu responded.

"Well," Serena sniffled and fought back her tears, "One of my officers went home wearing a buffet on his back. One officer was getting pummeled by a guy that I had to beat with my PR 24 just to get him off of her, one of my officers had to deal with a woman wielding a knife, and one of my officers had to diffuse a road rage incident. And all of this on the same day." She burst into tears.

"Wow. And I complain when my lunchmeat goes bad." Stu meant that as a way to lighten the mood, but like a train rolling off the rails, he crashed and burned. "How can I help?"

"Oh, I'm sorry. It's just been a hard week. I have such good officers who never complain. I wish I could do something for them," Serena replied.

"Okay. Let's do something for them. Let's plan a get-together with them here at the house. Those on duty can swing by during the course of their patrols. What do you think?" asked Stu.

"Yea. We can grill burgers, heat up some baked beans, a salad, some fruit, some strawberry shortcake, a few beers for those off duty and some soda pop for those on duty, and whatever else we can think of. When?" asked Serena.

"How about a week from Saturday? Start about 5:30 and keep it going until everyone has had a chance to enjoy," Stu replied. "Now, in the meantime, let's get dressed up and go to dinner and dancing," Stu offered.

"Okay, sounds like fun. What should I wear?"

"Surprise me, babe," Stu responded.

An hour later, Serena appeared in her living room where Stu was patiently waiting.

"Wow! You, Wow!" That's all he could get out.

Serena was very excited about his reaction. She was wearing a red minidress, red high heels, dangly earrings, and sexy-smelling perfume.

"Wow! Absolutely beautiful! Amazing!" Stu seemed to be head-over-heels crazy about the way his fiancé looked and found it impossible to peel his eyes away from her.

"Oh, my," Serena responded. "You ought to go away for ten days more often!"

By this time, Stu was on his feet. He grabbed her forcefully by her waist, drew her into him, and began kissing her neck. He was gentle and romantic.

Serena swooned. "We better go, Stu, honey. If we stay, we will find ourselves in temptation nation."

Stu laughed at this. "Temptation nation! Where do you come up with this stuff?"

"I guess I just go with the flow. By the way, you look good enough to bite," Serena said provocatively.

The evening's dinner and dancing served as a romantic reminder of how each felt about the other. In fact, the whole weekend served that purpose.

"My goodness," Stu said the following evening, "you look good in blue jeans as well. On Sunday morning, Stu complimented her on the shorts she wore around the house. "Is there anything you can't wear that you make look so good? Let's hurry up and get married!"

Serena felt like a princess. She was never made to feel that way before, and laughed when other women felt that way, but now she understood it. *The power of words from the man I love is so exhilarating*, she thought.

"Let's discuss your upcoming test. When do you take it, and when do you find out the results?" asked Serena.

I will take it Tuesday afternoon at 1:30. It's a state exam available for all biologists who are qualified and interested in the position. Probably won't get the results for a week to ten days," explained Stu. "The one who scores highest gets the offer. If he or she turns it down, then they offer the position to number 2, and so on."

"So you need to be number one. No pressure there," Serena commented. "Have you been able to study yet?" asked a confused Serena.

"No, honey, you don't study for it. It's a test of what you know. I have no idea what's on the test, so…" His voice dropped off.

"I see," said Serena. "So, if you score the highest, you'll be offered the position in Walker. Same hours and basically the same field work," Serena was working it out in her head.

"Yep. And I'll accept immediately," Stu responded. "Hey, let's take a walk in the park. Put on those sexy jeans of yours," Stu stated seductively, adding a 'woo-hoo' sound at the end.

"What has gotten into you, Stu? All these compliments."

"I don't know. I just am eager to marry you and start our lives together," Stu explained.

Arriving at the park, Stu asked, "So, when do you want to start having kids?"

Serena gulped. "Well, I think we first need to determine what we will do about childcare, you know, when I go back to work," replied Serena.

"Yep, I understand. I don't like the idea of putting our children in a daycare facility. I'd rather pay a good friend or a dependable relative. How about you?"

"I agree. But that doesn't leave us with many available options," explained Serena. "All our family members are hours away."

"Well, we do have time to figure that out. A couple of years, right?"

"Correct, Stu. We do have time, and who knows what will happen by the time we're ready?"

"Well, I suppose I had better start on my way back home. I've got a full day tomorrow and an exam on Tuesday afternoon."

They made their way back to Serena's home. Stu ate a quick, small lunch, and made his way to his car.

"I'll be back Friday night. Don't forget, party on Saturday night," Stu reminded her. "Have a fantastic and safe week!"

15
Cage This Bird

The week was passing by quite quickly. Serena was excited after her weekend with Stu, and especially the romantic dates she had been enjoying with him. Late night dancing, long walks in the park, and the compliments Stu had been passing out like Halloween candy. He especially loved her red mini dress, her little shorts, and of all things, how she looked in her jeans. Serena could tell something was on Stu's mind; maybe they had just turned a corner in their relationship and had taken it to the next level. Either way, Serena was pleased with all the attention and affection Stu was showering on her. She had never seen him quite like this. She admitted she liked this romantic side of him. The conversation was more and more focused on getting married. Serena could only hope that in forty years Stu would feel the same way about her.

She daydreamed about the hours spent in Stu's strong arms, how he made her feel safe when he wrapped her in his muscular arms. She dreamt of the hour-long sessions on the couch, just kissing each other and barely coming up for air. She imagined two little kids, hers and Stu's, running around the house and laughing while mommy and daddy chased them. She could hardly contain herself as she imagined saying "I do" at her wedding.

Thursday morning, Sgt. Morris finished her morning briefing with her officers. She jumped into her squad car and drove away from the precinct. Her thoughts were still focused on Stu and her pending marriage. She didn't know why she was so happy this morning, especially since her wedding plans were still the same. Whose career would end? Whose house would they live in? When would they start a family? Could they make ends meet on one income? These questions were the same ones yet to be reconciled. She decided she would make a point to watch each of her officers in action today. She had hoped to observe from a small distance each officer issuing a traffic citation, or giving someone a warning, or directing traffic, or whatever would come up that she could observe and provide constructive feedback. It was going well when at about 2 p.m. she responded to a call from a local store regarding a shoplifter. This kept her tied up for a solid twenty minutes as she watched the videotape from store security.

Suddenly, a call broadcasted over her hand-held radio: "Shots fired. Location, the top tier of the parking garage on Mendell Avenue."

You have got to be kidding me! thought Sgt. Morris.

Officer Rodriguez was the first to respond with Officer Barnes broadcasting she would back up Rodriguez. Rodriguez was about two minutes away and Barnes about three and a half miles out. Sgt. Morris called for an available unit to transport the shoplifter to the city jail. Officer Helmsley responded he would be there in three minutes.

By the time Sgt. Morris was free, she heard over the radio that Officer Rodriguez and Barnes were exchanging fire with the perpetrator.

"It's Fitz," Rodriguez, yelled into the radio microphone.

Sgt. Morris was racing to the scene, now in total disbelief. *How is Fitz involved in this?*

Officer Barnes then broadcasted an update. "Rodriguez and I have suspect surrounded on two sides. We are behind our squad cars exchanging shots with Fitz. He is behind his vehicle as well."

"Stay low and stay alert," responded Sgt. Morris over the air, "be there shortly."

The chief, who had been in his office, heard the commotion over the police radio and launched himself like a rocket ship out of his office and into his unmarked squad car. He sped to the scene, lights flashing and siren wailing, and arrived just seconds before Sgt. Morris. He took up position on the third side of suspect Fitz and drew his weapon on Fitz as well. Sgt. Morris rolled up and assessed the situation and took position with the chief behind his squad car. When Fitz realized he was surrounded on three sides, with no chance of escape, he thew his firearm to the ground and raised his hands high in the air. Sgt. Morris told Barnes to hold her position and cover Rodriguez. She then told Fitz to lay down on the ground with hands spread over his head. He complied. She then instructed Rodriguez to holster his firearm and retrieve Fitz's firearm from the ground.

As Rodriguez was making his way to recover the weapon, Sgt. Morris heard the chief whisper to her, "As soon as he is secured, you send your officers away, and then give me five minutes alone with him before we take him to the station!"

"Chief, holster your weapon, please," said Sgt. Morris.

Fitz's weapon now recovered, Officers Rodriguez and Barnes cuffed Fitz, stood him up, searched him for weapons, and then read him his rights.

"We'll put him in my car," whispered the chief.

Sgt. Morris approached Fitz, who told her that he was just doing what he was paid to do.

"Who's paying you for what?" demanded Sgt. Morris.

"Mrs. Sanderson."

It took a moment for this name to compute in Sgt. Morris' brain. And then it registered. Sanderson. Mother of Melony Sanderson who shot Willy. Sgt. Morris took Fitz into her custody and told Rodriguez and Barnes to pick up Mrs. Sanderson. Both officers drove off quickly to the last known address of Mrs. Sanderson.

Chief Breckenridge, unaware of the conversation between Fitz and Sgt. Morris, saw only one thing. He saw that Sgt. Morris was walking Fitz to the squad car and all other officers had disappeared. He smiled and thought to himself, *Finally, I can give this guy the beating he deserves!*

"Just bring him around to the back of my car, Sergeant," the chief demanded.

Instead, Sgt. Morris escorted Fitz to the back of her patrol car and closed the door behind him. She drove away with Fitz without saying a word to the chief. The chief just stared her down as she drove away. She radioed the station and informed dispatch she would need detectives for an interrogation.

Sgt. Morris and the chief arrived at the station at the same time. Sgt. Morris, fearful of how her failure to obey a direct order from the chief would affect her career, stepped out of her vehicle. The chief was out of his vehicle and was making his way directly to her.

"Chief, it's over. We've got Fitz in a cage for a long time," Sgt. Morris pleaded. "He's a caged bird!"

The chief stared at Sgt. Morris and breathed heavily. Anger was prevalent in his expression as well as his body language. There was nothing more the chief could do at this point. Deep down, he understood that Sgt. Morris did everything correctly and followed procedure and protocol, thereby protecting him and the department. But this didn't make it any easier. He had his heart set on revenge and wouldn't be able to get it. All he wanted was a couple of minutes alone with Fitz to drive home his point and his fists. All he wanted was to mess up Fitz's life like Fitz messed up his. All he wanted was to rearrange Fitz's face!

Sgt. Morris took Fitz into the precinct's interrogation room. Detective Roskam was present and prepared to interrogate Fitz. He took Sgt. Morris' statement in private first and then asked everyone to clear the interrogation room.

"Sorry, Chief, that includes you," said Detective Roskam.

Begrudgingly, the chief left the room.

16

And Then Cage the Lie

"So Fitz, we meet again. What the heck are you doing shooting at police officers?"

"I'm not speaking," Fitz brazenly responded.

"Okay, we have Ma Sanderson in the room next door. I'm quite sure she'll talk."

"Be sure to ask her about the $70,000."

"What about the 70 grand?" Roskam asked.

"The 70 grand she promised to pay me!" Fitz replied.

"For what? What did you have to do for that?"

"That's all I'm saying."

"Okay, I'll be right back," Roskam replied.

He left the room and entered the room next door where Ma Sanderson was being held. "Tell me about the 70 grand," Roskam asked Ma Sanderson.

"Huh! 70 grand! He thinks I promised to pay him 70 grand for keeping my son from murdering the officer who arrested my daughter, Melony."

"Yea, I remember that. You gave Fitz a note asking him to protect your son, Mark. To keep him from exacting revenge on one of our officers," said Roskam.

"That's right. He went rogue and decided he was going to kill a cop to get revenge for his sister. Can I go now? I was told I was just wanted for questioning."

"So, the 70 grand was to protect Mark?" asked Roskam.

"Do I look like I have 70 grand? I've never even seen 70 grand," Ma Sanderson argued.

Detective Roskam left the room and reentered the interrogation room which held Fitz. "She knows nothing about 70 grand," Roskam said, "so tell me what the money was for."

"It figures she'd deny it. I'm not saying anything. You want me to talk, then bring in Serena. I'd like to talk to her," Fitz demanded.

"You don't demand anything. I say what's happening in here," retorted Roskam.

"Okay. Your park, your rules. As for me, my lips are zipped!"

The room was silent for a long time.

Finally, Roskam broke the silence, "I've got all night."

"As long as I'm in police custody, I do too!" replied Fitz.

Two hours later, Roskam brought Sgt. Morris into the interrogation room.

"What do you want, Fitz?" she asked.

"Just one thing, Serena. I want to know why you turned me down cold. All I wanted was to talk to you, to ask you some questions."

"In the same way you wanted the chief's wife to answer these same questions. Your attempt to get involved with Sgt. Morris and your involvement with Sue Ann was strictly business, a way to facilitate your plan," Roskam interrupted.

A long pause ensued before Sgt. Morris broke the silence.

"Here's your chance, Fitz. Ask away."

"Too late now. It's over!" replied Fitz.

"What's over?" asked Detective Roskam.

"The whole thing. It's done," replied Fitz.

Serena left the room at Roskam's hand motion.

"Look, you're going down for attempted murder on police officers no matter if you talk or not. The question is whether you want to take the fall alone," Roskam continued. "Let's start with the note you received from Ma Sanderson a while back. She was hiring you to prevent her son, Mark, from murdering Officer Rodriguez. Is that correct?"

"Yea, something like that," replied Fitz.

"And you were to be paid 70 grand for that?" asked Roskam.

"Yep."

"Seems a little steep," Roskam concluded.

"She's good for it. She's loaded," Fitz responded.

"I see. And where did she get all this money?" asked Roskam.

"I don't know. I just know she's good for it and a whole lot more."

"Okay. So, you prevented the murder, but Mark is in prison. Is that why she refuses to pay you the 70 grand?" asked Roskam skeptically.

"She isn't paying me because the job isn't finished," Fitz responded coolly.

"So, to earn that 70 grand, she required you to do something else?" asked Roskam.

"Yes. I was attempting to finish her request, but now it's over."

"So the note was a charade?" asked Roskam.

"The note was to give to her other son, Donald. I was to find him and give him the note, warning him not to interfere with Mark, whom she realized would do anything to get revenge," Fitz replied.

He realized that Roskam was beginning to figure this out. He knew it was just a matter of time. His question of whether he wanted to take the fall alone had registered with Fitz.

"I see. I see," said Detective Roskam. "So, the note was a fraud."

"Yea, it was simply a way to accomplish her will," responded Fitz.

"And you were to find Donald and give him the note, which in turn would pave the way for Mark, who ultimately failed in his attempt. Is this correct?"

"Yea, you got it," Fitz replied.

"Where are you currently living?" asked Roskam. "We know you don't live in Apt. 107."

"I live in the basement of Helen Sanderson," Fitz boldly stated.

"Excuse me for a minute," said Roskam. He exited the room and entered the other interrogation room. "One question, Mrs. Sanderson. When did you get Fitz involved in your plan? Did he know about from the beginning, or did you let him in after Mark was sent to prison?"

"That dumb ass. Why is he talking?" Helen Sanderson asked out loud to herself.

"Listen, Mrs. Sanderson. You are implicated. There are no two ways about it. You are now under arrest," Detective Roskam stated.

He read her Miranda rights and then asked her if she wanted to talk. Helen Sanderson, at that moment, having come to the realization that her plan had failed and was transparent now to the police, confessed and confirmed what Roskam already knew.

Roskam called for both Fitz and Helen to be transported separately to the holding cells in the city jail. He then asked the chief into his office and shared his findings. For the first time, Chief Breckenridge understood that his wife's affair with Fitz was nothing more than a business deal for Fitz, without the knowledge of his wife. He was using her for information which she could not get because the affair was exposed so soon. It didn't excuse what she did, but it did clear up some doubts and questions in his mind, questions that up until now had been plaguing the chief.

As the chief exited the room, he recalled the words of Sgt. Morris. *Chief, we have caged the bird.*

"Yes, Serena, we have caged the bird," he said to himself, "and now we have caged the lie."

I need to get home and start repairing my marriage, he thought. *I have treated Sue Ann quite harshly. I need to share with her how I am feeling, and we need to get some marriage counseling.*

Once Breckenridge left the room, Roskam took a quick break. He needed to collect his thoughts in preparation for what he was planning next. He called for Sgt. Morris, Officer Rodriguez, and Officer Barnes.

It was time to let them in on this wretched plan gone wrong. It took about twenty minutes to gather everybody. Sgt. Morris and her crew were exhausted by this time. They were all looking forward to completing their paperwork and then to getting home. They sat in the briefing room and wrote their reports. The room was a bit rowdy as they exaggerated the day's events. It was good to vent in such a positive way. Each officer playfully presented him or herself as the hero of the incident. It was good, clean joking which had no bearing on their reports.

17
The Big Reveal

Everyone gathered in the interrogation room. Detective Roskam welcomed everyone as they entered the room, even to the point of shaking hands. Sgt. Morris was excited to hear what Roskam would divulge.

"Let me start by saying how proud I am of each and every one of you. What I am about to tell you was a long, well-thought-out process and series of events acted out by Mrs. Helen Sanderson, Mark Sanderson, Melony Sanderson, Donald Sanderson, and Fitz, a so-called private investigator," Roskam began. "You will all recall the day when Melony Sanderson shot down Willy in cold blood. Once she pulled the trigger, she fled in her vehicle but was subsequently picked up by Officer Rodriguez. She was sentenced to life in prison. A private investigator by the name of Grant Fitzgerald made his way into town and claimed he was working for a woman, but never gave the name of that woman or the nature of his business with her. We have come to learn that the woman employing him was Helen Sanderson, with whom he took up residence. Fitz was involved in the shooting incident on the day Officer Rodriguez was the target. Mark Sanderson, son of Helen, took it upon himself to attempt to carry out a murder plot against Rodriguez. That was the day Sgt Morris rammed her patrol car into the steel dumpster on the top level of the parking garage."

Everyone laughed and looked at Sgt. Morris.

"Suddenly, Fitz appeared out of nowhere, and shots were then fired from behind. These shots were from the gun of Donald Sanderson, the other son of Helen Sanderson, who maintained that he was firing at his brother Mark in order to prevent him from killing a police officer. You, Rodriguez," he pointed at Rodriguez. "The subsequent investigation revealed that Fitz was carrying a note, confirmed to have been written by Helen Sanderson, warning Donald to stay away from Mark as Mark was looking for revenge of his sister Melony's arrest, and was willing to kill anyone in his way. Helen Sanderson felt she had already lost a daughter to life in prison, and she didn't want to lose another child. So, she hired Fitz to find Donald Sanderson to warn him. She was unable to talk to Mark because Mark was on the run, or should I say, on the hunt, for Officer Rodriguez. Mark was refusing to talk to his mother. Everybody with me so far," Roskam asked.

Silence permeated the room until Sgt. Morris spoke up and said, "With you so far."

"Good," said Roskam, "then I will continue. Mark was arrested as was Donald, both were sentenced to prison. Ultimately, Helen Sanderson was arrested and given probation for her failure to notify the authorities of her son Mark's intentions. No charges were made against Fitz, so he was released. At some point in this mess, Fitz asked Sgt. Morris on a date."

All eyes stared at Sgt. Morris again.

"I said no," Sgt. Morris said sarcastically.

Again, laughter broke out in the room.

"Correct, but as it turns out, Fitz had no romantic interests. His interest in Sgt. Morris was strictly business. I'll get to that in a minute."

Roskam wanted to say the same thing about the chief's wife, but he decided it was better to keep that to himself rather than get rumors floating.

He continued, "That brings us to the most recent incident. Officer Barnes and Sgt. Morris responded to a call for back-up from Officer Rodriguez, who is now taking fire from Fitz. Understand, Fitz set this up and was waiting for the police to respond. He had his car positioned where and how he wanted it. He chose the location, one that he was very familiar with. He was behind his car in order to get maximum coverage from bullet spray. And once again, the first one to respond was Officer Rodriguez. Gunshots rang out between Fitz and Rodriguez. Once back-up arrived, Fitz felt he was a caged bird, surrounded on three sides by four officers. He threw down his weapon and surrendered. He realized at that point he was not getting his 70 thousand dollars!"

"70 grand!" Officer Rodriguez interjected. "70 grand? For what?"

"I'm getting to that. Fitz claimed it was promised to him by Helen Sanderson as payment for finding Donald and warning him to avoid Mark. Fitz further claimed that Helen was withholding this money because Mark was arrested, somehow blaming Fitz for not doing his job correctly," Roskam stated.

"That makes no sense," Sgt. Morris blurted. "He was hired to warn Donald, not to protect Mark."

"Right, but was he? That is the question. You see, each and every time dispatch called for shots fired on the top tier of the parking garage, it was Fitz who called dispatch. Every single time!"

"Well, sure. I guess that makes sense. He was hoping Rodriguez would show up, which in turn would cause Mark to show up, which in turn may lead to finding Donald," stated Officer Barnes.

"Nope," Roskam interrupted. "Not true. Fitz was calling dispatch for a different reason. He was collecting information. First, getting back to the information he wanted from Sgt. Morris when he asked her on a date. What he wanted to find out from Sgt. Morris was Officer Rodriguez's schedule. He wanted to be sure that the next time he called dispatch for 'shots fired' that Rodriguez was on duty and would be the first to respond. Everybody still tracking with me?"

"Yes."

"Yep."

"All good so far," the room resounded.

"Okay," Detective Roskam continued. "Now that we have the facts, let's look at what really happened!"

A silent pause hovered over the room.

"This whole incident was actually very well thought out. And had Helen Sanderson given Fitz the 70 grand, it may have worked out, or at least you may think that. But not true. You see, the 70 grand was meant as payment for something totally different. The notion that it was payment for finding Donald was nothing more than a cover story developed by Fitz and Helen. The note that Fitz was to give to Donald was also a cover story, also written by Helen, whose purpose was to protect Fitz as long as possible should things go wrong."

Roskam paused a few moments, giving time for everyone to process his words.

"And if you haven't figured it out by now, here is the big reveal. Helen, Mark, Donald, and Fitz were in this together the entire time. When Mark Sanderson was shooting at Rodriguez, Donald was also, from behind, under the cover of preventing the murder of Rodriguez. The reality was that each brother was attempting to get close enough to deliver the kill shot. And Fitz? Fitz's job was to isolate Rodriguez and assist the brothers in this murderous plan. He also had the green light from Helen to murder Rodriguez. He was waiting to take his shot but was first waiting for the Sanderson boys to attempt it themselves. The note he carried served to protect him and keep him from being implicated in this murderous plot. With the brothers in prison, and his lust for money, he then took his turn to murder Rodriguez."

So that's why after the trial Helen and Fitz nodded to each other. It all makes sense, now, Sgt. Morris thought.

"So, as it stands, Fitz and Helen have been arrested for conspiracy to commit murder and any other charges the attorney general can prove. Donald will be charged with conspiracy as well. And that leads me back to where I began this meeting. The teamwork displayed by this group; the leadership displayed by Sgt. Morris is a textbook example of how police work should pan out. Whether you know it or not, the fact that you all stood together, shoulder to shoulder, took a group of killers off the streets and into prison. Well done. Well done, Sergeant." Roskam shook hands with all of them. "Any questions? No? Okay. Well, allow me to say one last thing." He looked at Officer Rodriguez. "Officer Rodriguez, this is over! There is no more threat against your life. We have caught them all. I should say, this group of dedicated officers has put an end to this madness. You are safe from the Sanderson clan. The lies that were perpetrated by the Sandersons and Fitz are now caged, just like the liars. They can no longer roam free," Roskam said victoriously. "It is finished!"

18
The Aftermath

It took a week or so for Officer Rodriguez to process the whole "murder for hire" plot against him. He took time to visit with departmental psychology staff once again as he began to realize just how much danger he was in. This incident caused him to reevaluate whether he wanted to remain a police officer.

The party at Sgt. Morris' house was a much-needed distraction and a great bonding experience. All of Serena's officers managed to make an appearance and enjoyed some stress-free time together. Stuart was impressed with the quality of people that worked with Serena. Several officers pulled Stuart aside and expressed their love for Sgt. Morris. It was evident that Serena had a familial relationship with her crew. Serena was all smiles and enjoyed her party.

The chief showed up for the party as well. Sgt. Morris noted to Stuart that he seemed to be overly nice to her. The chief enjoyed spending some off duty time with the troops. When the time was right, he asked Sgt. Morris if he could talk to her in private. They stepped inside and sat at the kitchen table.

"Serena, first of all I want to congratulate you. Your decision-making throughout this whole incident was outstanding and beyond reproach. You kept it professional, even when I didn't. I also want to say thanks. You never engaged in gossip with anybody, nor did you judge me. I did learn something from this. I have decided to make a few visits to the Departmental psychologist. I obviously need some practice in controlling my anger. The last thing I need is to embarrass myself or the department. I will get the help needed. Thanks for that," the chief stated politely.

"You are welcome, Chief. That's the least I could have done for you. Come on, let's get back to the party."

The following week, Stuart received the promotional test results. He called Serena and told her he scored number two. While this was a great score, both realized this may pose another obstacle with their wedding plans. Serena congratulated Stu on his good score. Stu explained that he hoped to know in a couple days whether the person first on the list had accepted the promotion. He saw that the number one biologist lived way south, so there was a chance that he would not accept the promotion, especially if he had a wife with a job and kids.

Serena was on pins and needles waiting for Stu to tell her who would get the promotion. That's all she thought about during her shift. Finally, her phone rang. It was Stu.

"Hi, Serena. Will you still marry me?"

"Oh, no, what happened?" asked a worried Serena.

"Well, I can put my home up for sale!"

"Really?" Serena gasped. "The other guy didn't take the promotion?"

"No. Turns out his wife was just promoted in her job a couple of months ago, and she is making good money. Neither one of them wanted to pass it up, so he turned down the promotion."

Serena screamed with joy. "I am so happy, Stu!"

"Me, too. But you haven't answered me," Stu responded.

"What, Honey, what?"

"Will you still marry me?"

"Of course, I will. I love you, Stu!"